ALSO BY EPHINY GALE

Collected short fiction

Next Curious Thing

Collected stage plays

The Playbook: Six Plays and One Libretto

PICK YOUR POTION

EPHINY GALE

*For Joy,
who listened to and
typed up my first stories*

CONTENTS

INTRODUCTION

In a nearby city, there is a set of forest-green double doors that nobody else seems to notice.

Passing through the doors, the sounds of the city fade and you find yourself in a comfortable bar. To your right, a group in their late teens or early twenties cluster around a board game. A middle-aged couple murmurs quietly to each other in a booth in the far corner. The carpet is a deep, plush purple and the seating all matches the green of the exterior doors. You hear laughter through an arch at the back; although this first area is only a modest size, the establishment seems to wind on and on like a labyrinth.

To the left is the bar counter, with hundreds of bottles stacked behind it in all shapes and colours. There are liquids in neon and pastel and some that glow in the semi-dark. Some of them are bubbling, and some seem to be smoking through holes in their lids.

The figure manning the bar gestures for you to choose a bar stool. This appears to be a thirty-something woman with odd hair, some of which has curled itself into ringlets and some of which is almost straight. She slides across a crimson menu: Pick Your Potion is debossed on the front.

THE MENU

Contains mild spoilers for the stories within.

CurioQueens

Baileys Irish Cream, earl grey tea, honeycomb syrup. Served with maple syrup candies.

I wrote this story when I was especially excited about real-life board games (which I still very much enjoy) and wanted to dream up a magical one. I grew up with media like *Jumanji* and *Yu-Gi-Oh*, but surprisingly few stories about magical board or card games seem to have been written since. I would love to see more!

This story, along with "The Orchard", gave me my first opportunity to attend the Aurealis Awards as a finalist. The awards ceremony was held purely online during the pandemic, but it still felt like such a treat to join via video and to have my work acknowledged on a national scale.

Restoration

Vodka, vanilla essence, soda water.

This one was written for a contest with the theme of "Ice" and where entries could be no more than 200 words. Many thanks to the person who commented and said this was the best story he'd read all year. I consider it to be the best microfiction I've ever written.

The Magic in Our Hands

House beer, cough syrup, frozen raspberries.

This is the third story I've written about hands (the others being "In the Beginning, All Our Hands Are Cold" and "Sickly Sweet"). It's kind of my brand now. Perhaps one day I will have enough for an entire collection themed around hands!

As well as a story about hands, this is also a story heavily inspired by my time in university student politics.

The image of the crystals embedded in hands came to me in a dream, along with the façade of the Hawthorn House of Mental Magic, and I ran with them from there.

All the Times I'm Ten
Milk, toffee ice cream, crumbled chocolate cookies. Served with a slice of carrot cake.

As a general rule, I tend to find the chosen one trope a little dull, so I wanted to play with it and find a way to twist it into a shape I found interesting, unexpected and exciting again.

Nowhere, Australia
Ginger beer, orange liqueur, soda water. Served with a slice of lemon.

I spent the first thirty-two years of my life living in the city, and then my wife and I bought a house in regional Australia. I was surprised by how quickly I felt at home in the country, but there were still many changes I needed to get used to.

This story was written about six months after we moved, while my wife was overseas and I was alone in the house in the middle of winter. Most of my stories are written on a laptop, but this one was written entirely on my phone over several nights, because there was always a cat on my lap instead.

The Candle Queen
Rose and jasmine tea, lavender syrup, salt. Served over a burning tea light.

Sometimes two good ideas will collide and morph into something better. For "The Candle Queen" these were a) an image of a girl with a crown of burning, dripping candles on her head, and b) a girl who couldn't ever be woken, otherwise the world would end.

This particular collision occurred halfway through my commute home, and I experienced a burst of energy and wrote the first few hundred words on my phone on the train.

Solace

Cherry-flavoured iced green tea, a sugared rim. Served with a side of chicken-salted popcorn.

I don't usually write stories set in space, so when I was approached to write one in a shared universe set on a spaceship called The Brahma, I knew I was in for a challenge. I'm very happy with how this one turned out, though, and I appreciate the feedback Pete Wood and Carol Scheina provided to shape it into the form it's in today.

The fashion design elements of this story were inspired by some of the old seasons of Project Runway that my wife and I were watching at the time.

Last Text

Coffee, manuka honey, a dash of milk.

For years, I had the idea of someone receiving the last texts people sent before they were murdered, and I didn't know what to do with it. It seemed like that was primarily a crime plot, and I am not a crime writer. Then one night, I was watching an episode of RuPaul's Drag Race, and to my delight most of this story suddenly came together.

Many thanks to Erin Cashier for suggesting the method of death that I utilise at the end of this piece, when I was struggling to pinpoint a method that would work but that wasn't "car accident".

La Vie En Mer

Apple cider, sliced strawberries, a salted rim.

I had wanted to write a cruise ship story for a long time. Then in 2022 or 2023 I saw some ads for a luxury residential cruise ship, which seemed like the perfect launch pad. Other inspirations for "La Vie En Mer" include the TV show *Sliders* and Carmen Maria Machado's "Especially Heinous: 272 Views of Law & Order SVU", which also tells a story using the synopses of TV episodes.

Rewind

Hot blueberry tea, lychee liqueur, rum. Served with rosemary.

I wrote this on New Year's Day. In the days prior, I had dreamt most of the scenes for this story and quite liked the parts my subconscious had given me, but they seemed so disjointed. I needed to work out how to make something story-shaped. Once I realised that I didn't have to tell this one front-to-back, everything fell into place.

Overnight, a Forest Grew

T2 Melbourne Breakfast tea, a dash of milk, a slice of lemon. Served along with a sausage in bread (with tomato sauce and mustard).

This is the most Australian story I've ever written – even more so than the one with "Australia" in the title! Although I often set my fiction in a subtly Australian location (e.g. the references to Bunnings in "Traces of Us, Hot Enough for Dinner") the City of Literature Office who generously commissioned this piece asked for it to be solidly placed in Melbourne, so I enjoyed adding in a lot more Australian and Melbournian references than I usually do.

The title of this piece, plus the narrator's "name" are references to my favourite picture book, *Where the Wild Things Are*.

Watchhouse

Gin, tonic water, elderflower liqueur, lime juice.

Please exercise caution with this one, as out of all my stories it seems to have the most capacity to upset and disturb people.

I was so pleased when The Dread Machine accepted this for publication, and even more thrilled when they used it as the inspiration for the gorgeous cover of the issue that "Watchhouse" appears in.

Light and Sleek and Strong
Rum, cola, lemon juice, a slice of orange. Served with wrapped boiled candies.

This is the result of daydreaming in the shower. It's weirder than I remember. Sorry?

Faewild
Pineapple juice, vodka, mint, soda water.

My love letter to the monster taming and creature collection genre. As a child, Pokémon was one of my favourite franchises, and I still love it 25+ years later as an adult. I've played many of the monster taming games out there (and would recommend *Pokémon Legends: Arceus* and the original *Yo-Kai Watch* as two of the best).

I wanted "Faewild" to capture the magic and wonder that this genre does so well, while not shying away from some of the more dark and adult elements that arose as I was writing this.

The White Factory
Sprite, soda water, Life Savers Duos Gummy Rings.

While I was in primary school, I occasionally caught an episode of a children's gameshow called *A*mazing*, and I was mesmerised. Wikipedia tells me there were other elements to the show as well, but all I remember are the segments where the contestants had to race through an elaborate, colourful maze searching for hidden keys.

Anyway, this is a story about running around a warren of rooms and searching for hidden rings.

Neuro
Coconut water, blended strawberries, mandarin juice, mint leaves.

For most of my twenties, every few months I would dream a detailed stage musical, and when I woke I could remember some of the visuals and music – for about 20 seconds. Then it was gone. The music my unconscious created was so complex and enjoyable, and I always felt a significant loss that I couldn't hang onto those songs in my waking life.

The two key inspirations for this piece were 1) those dream musicals, and 2) my regular ingestion of YouTube videos.

This story idea had been percolating for a while when Tehani Croft kindly invited me to submit something to be considered for *The Art of Being Human* anthology, which finally prompted me to actually write it. Luckily, Tehani and fellow editor Stephanie Lai enjoyed "Neuro" as much as I was hoping they would, and they accepted it for the anthology.

When the Ice Comes In
Spherical ice cubes, peppermint syrup, cinnamon, soda water.

When I sat down to write this piece, I knew I wanted to write a modern climate change story inspired by "The Little Match Girl," but the only thing I could remember about that was an image of a small girl holding a lit match and matchbox in the snow. I decided to write anyway. After I'd finished "When the Ice Comes In" I looked up the original "Little Match Girl" and was pleasantly surprised by all the similarities between them.

Smol Animaux
Orange juice, lemon juice, sparkling white wine. Served with a shot of coffee on the side.

My pandemic story, partially written at the 2023 Bendigo Writers' Festival once we were able to travel again, some time after Melbourne's long lockdowns had finished.

Vaguely inspired by Neopets.

The Most Powerful Witch in Witchville
Aniseed syrup, caffeinated lemonade, whole blueberries. Served with a side of gingerbread.

After waking up with this title in my head, the associated story idea came together very quickly.

I sometimes write to story-specific music playlists, but this is the only time where I've associated a song with a story so strongly years later. In my mind, the scene in "Witchville" with the metal spiders will forever be set to "Tear You Apart" by She Wants Revenge.

This is (Not) My Beautiful Cat
Lactose-free milk, lactose-free vanilla ice cream, apple syrup, vanilla wafers.

For all the cats I've loved.

Lovely Lilas
Passionfruit juice, orange juice, blended raspberries, lemonade, a slice of lime.

Throughout the course of my life, several different people have told me that I'm the nicest person they've ever met. I wondered how technology might want to leverage that.

The Orchard
Hot cinnamon tea, honey, cranberry juice.

Shortly after Trump had been elected, I deliberately sat down to write something warm, gentle and cosy. No-one's life or livelihood is in danger. Everyone is having a nice time competing for a magical orchard.

Because I needed to create so many different types of magical trees for this story, I often consulted a couple of packs of illustrated Dixit cards for inspiration for them. More magical trees. More. So many.

Inheritance
Lemonade, lime juice, bitters, soda water, lemon slices, lime slices.

Another story written for a contest where entries could be no more than 200 words, this time with the theme of "Haunted". This piece was awarded second place.

Marina, Hel and Cady Save the Universe
Billson's Fairy Floss Cordial, vodka, soda water, mandarin juice. Served with a chewy choc-chip cookie.

There are a thousand things I love about my wife. A small selection includes her humour, her fierce intelligence, her passion, her dedication, her straightforwardness, her trustworthiness, her honesty... I could go on a long time. About 18 months after we married she was diagnosed with autism, and I realised that so many of the things that I love about her were at least partly *because of* her autism, and that it was something to deeply appreciate.

There aren't many autistic love interests represented in the media – a real shame, because autistic people can make incredible partners. Hopefully this story is a tiny step in the right direction. The girls in this story are also loosely inspired by my friendship group in high school (many of whom have grown up to get ADHD and/or autism diagnoses in adulthood) and this would have been the perfect story for me to read at 16.

Many thanks to my wife for performing a sensitivity read on this story. She is an incredibly talented novelist and editor, and I'm very grateful that she's happy to be the first reader for my writing.

Like Marina, I'm probably not entirely neurotypical, either.

As Long as We Both Shall Live and After, Too
Coffee, ice, cookies and cream ice cream, vanilla essence.

If anyone is concerned that a lot of queer women die young in my stories, please understand: in my personal experience, they do.

Traces of Us, Hot Enough for Dinner
Sparkling rosé, pomegranate juice, fresh raspberries.

Time loops are one of my favourite story tropes; "Traces of Us..." is my sapphic time loop story, and one of my favourite things I've ever written.

The parts of this piece set at a wedding were informed by the nine months I spent working as a professional wedding DJ. The poem is one I wrote during a break in a Master of Arts Management tutorial when I was twenty.

This story was a finalist at the Aurealis Awards after our lockdowns had eased, and my excuse to go to those awards in person for the first time, which I'll always remember fondly.

END OF MENU

"Choose one or two, or order them all," says the bartender. "I'm here all night."

\-   Ephiny Gale, 2024

CURIOQUEENS

The very first time I play, I am eleven. My parents are collectors and connoisseurs of magical artefacts, although 90 percent of these are completely inert. The latest one, however, is not.

I am, in the strictest terms, Not Allowed to Touch It, but I can't remember anything I've ever wanted more, and my parents have never been very good at following through with punishments. I convince my father to go horse riding and wear him out. I steal the key from the inside of his boot while he is sleeping.

My mother catches me cross-legged on the storeroom table, stroking the most beautiful game board I have ever seen. She says that if I'm going to insist on playing, that she'll play with me, because the most dangerous way to play is with someone who doesn't love you.

The board is solid and three-dimensional. It looks rectangular from above, but from the side it resembles a stretched-out witch's hat with a flattened tip. Along the top, the name CURIOQUEENS is engraved in large capital letters, and underneath that: *A game of trust*. The entire board is made from expensive crystal, opaque in the middle and transparent on the "brim" where the cards are placed. "So the board can read what cards you've played," says my mother.

She explains the rules as follows:

1. You will receive 10 cards and must play five.

2. Most of the 300 possible cards are good cards, with positive or neutral effects like "Never have the flu again," or "your hair turns permanently blue." However, about 20 percent of the pack are bad cards that will cause the players harm.

3. Some of the cards will affect you, some will affect your opponent, and some can do either depending on which way you orient them on the board.

4. Approximately a third of the cards are whisper cards, which means that you can't tell your opponent what they are or the game will break your fingers and sew your lips shut.

5. Looking at the cards outside of playing the game, or not completing a game once it has begun, will be punished.

I stare at my mother then, and she says, "So you can't relax your arm and let me see your hand, like you sometimes do by accident. Do you still want to play?"

I do, so she reaches out and pulls a hair from the back of my neck, which is tradition, and ties it around a small post next to the CURIOQUEENS letters. Once I've done the same with her hair on the opposite post, there is a barely perceptible humming, and then the game serves us each 10 cards from the slots that open halfway up the board.

The cards are all backed with gold foil, and I pick them up reverently.

My first task is to read all the cards carefully and sort the good cards from the bad cards. I have three of the bad cards — I move them to the back of my fan. This is easy!

"It might be easy today," says Mother, "but it wouldn't be easy if you had more than five of the bad cards."

"That's unlikely, though," I say, puzzling over whether I would rather be 7 percent more beautiful or 7 percent better at maths.

"Unlikely, but far from impossible."

I start laying my chosen cards face-down in their crystal slots, making extra sure that my mother can't see.

My mother is holding up one card in particular. "Would you like to meet your soulmate in five years under an oak tree?"

At sunrise on the same date, exactly five years later, I hurry down to the oak tree a kilometre or two from the house. I am wearing one of my best dresses, lilac with embroidered white roses, and Mother has curled the ends of my hair. I have a heavy picnic basket to share with my future husband when he arrives.

I watch the morning stream of people and horses, women with baskets across their shoulders and boys flicking the sleep crusts from their eyes. I pay precise attention to all the young gentlemen that pass. None of them pause to speak with me. Some of them glance at my dress, or smile; I wonder if that counts as us meeting.

By lunchtime I am nestled between the roots of the tree, chewing on a cracker. Surely my soulmate will not miss a few biscuits.

And then it is sunset, and many of the people I saw in the morning are coming back the way they came. I try to keep myself pretty, my skirts arranged neatly around my knees and my eyes pinned to the road. There are still plenty of hours left to meet my soulmate, and the game has never been wrong before.

A girl about my age asks why I've been fixed to the same spot all day. I offer her a truthful explanation, but I don't dare pry my eyes away from the men on the road. She returns after dark with a blanket and a flask of hot cocoa. She keeps me patient company into the night.

We wake up together the next day, underneath the woollen blanket, propped against each other and the tree trunk. I see her face properly for the first time and feel the universe slightly realign.

"Oh," I say.

And she has the most radiant smile.

The girl's name is Mina, and we marry during my twentieth year. We braid orchid flowers into each other's hair and jump from ropes into lakes and keep no secrets from each other, save the ones from CurioQueens that keep safe our mouths and hands.

We only play the game twice, once during our engagement and once not long after our wedding (the first time, I gain an advantage in creating good first impressions; the second time I lose both my little toes). Mother managed to imbue me with a healthy respect for the game's dangers, but it follows me around. It seems that "my fondest medium-sized wish" from when I was eleven was to be able to play CurioQueens whenever I liked, and the game manifests this by appearing within reaching distance whenever I wake, regardless of where I may have left it the night before. In my jokes my board is my faithful hound, and on occasion I tap it gently on its title like a pet.

Until the day that Mina never comes home.

She is found ten minutes' walk from her flower shop, crushed by a bolting horse, daffodils and carnations flattened into her bruised skin like decoupage. When I finally see her, my own skin pales until it almost matches her deathly white.

I check the date in my diary with shaking hands. It is not long past our second wedding anniversary, and thus well within the realms of possibility.

From previous experience, I know there is a whisper card in the CurioQueens deck marked with *You will die two years from today*, and that may be pointed towards either of the players. I am struck with the deep and terrible knowledge of something I can never prove, and in that moment I both fervently love and hate my Mina with equal measure.

My mother and I take honeycomb tea in her upstairs drawing room. I am still in my funeral clothes, with the veil pinned back so that it does not drip into my teacup.

"But what would the rest of her hand have been," I say, "to make her choose that card."

My mother is chopping an éclair into several equal sections with a fork. "You'll never know that, Victoria. The important thing is that she protected you. You made the right decision, playing with someone who loved you more than she loved herself."

My eyes are defocusing. I place my own half-eaten macaron back on the coffee table.

Her cutlery clinks on the china. "You recall how I told you what the CurioQueens games were made for?"

"Perhaps." I have a vague memory of her telling me this years ago, back before I'd even met Mina. "They were presents to foreign royals, their courts and other influential people. For diplomacy."

"It was presented as diplomacy, certainly." Out of the corner of one eye, I see my mother spear a section of éclair with her miniature fork. "But that's not the generally accepted understanding now, and certainly not the one that your father and I subscribe to. Those games are weapons."

She waits for me to properly hold her gaze before she continues: "Please don't play again."

I trade my widow's skirts for saddle pants. I pack my horse light. I do not bring the CurioQueens board, though of course it will follow me anywhere. I tell myself I don't have a destination in mind, that I simply wish to get away. And then my first morning alone in an inn, my fingers skim the crystal edges of the board, and all of the fresh shallow cuts on my hands make the deep cuts inside of me a little easier to bear.

I carry the board downstairs. This inn is like any other inn. The woman/man/boy/girl behind the bar allows me to sell my services for a 10 percent cut, my services being a play of the enchanted game of legendary kings and queens. The privilege doesn't come cheaply. No sir/ma'am, I don't ever play myself, just like a wine merchant never samples his finest wares.

I sit on a bench nearby while they play, watching their scarred bodies heal, watching sapphire rings materialize on bony fingers. Watching careless young men break their hands and howl through lips sewn with heavy twine. After the second time this happens, I have a small pair of scissors in my breast pocket to hand to their partners. I watch players weep with happiness or horror and worry about the state of my soul, coiling like an electric blue spirit inside my chest, and then I take another sip of the spirit in my glass. I don't stay to watch longer-term; I'm never in any one place for more than two nights.

A bitter winter follows a mild autumn, but I have very few concerns. If my board is ever stolen, which it is occasionally, it always returns to my side. Losing my money is more of an inconvenience, but I have extra secreted away while I travel, and it's always easy to make some more. The greatest annoyance comes from losing my horse or the banner I hang behind me when I sell my games. After one customer received an especially severe batch of cards, I suppose I was lucky to get away with a ripped banner and a few punches to the jaw.

More than once, players will read their hands and walk away from the board entirely, unheeding my shouted warnings. Their hearts stopped before they even left the inn.

But I never force anyone to play, and I tell them all the rules upfront, and not all of the reactions towards me are negative. Sometimes, an elated girl or boy will throw themselves towards me, dizzy about achieving their dreams on a good draw, and I'll retire to my room early with full pockets and an attractive bedmate. They've won themselves a love match or their mobility back or an enviable singing voice. "Just don't play again," I whisper into their ears as they wrap their legs around me, and they laugh.

In the early spring I share a town with some other nomadic visitors, the circus and theatre troupe *The Marvelous Striped Magicians*, and take the evening off to wander through their venue. The red stripes on the heavy linen of their tents ripple in the wind, and the smell of candy apples and spiced cider floats around me like music. I buy a cone of maple syrup candies from a girl painted with rainbow clouds, no older than ten. I see the fire twirlers and blade swallowers, watch their production of *The Angels of Fleecewood* and have my fortune read by a tattooed woman covered in inked dice. "You shall have a wealthy and lonely life," she says, and then it is my turn to laugh.

I am the last one in the acrobats' tent at the end of the night, having tossed a few coins onto the empty stage and taking my time to finish off my maple candy. Just as I'm about to rise, one of the acrobats drops back into the centre of the tent. She bobs upside down, suspended by elastics, her long brown hair twice dusting the pale wood of the floor. "Ma'am," she says, "while we appreciate your patronage, you can't stay here forever."

"I was just leaving."

"Wait," she says, hooking her finger for me to come closer, although it looks odd upside down. "Aren't you the lady from *The Garfont* earlier today? With the cursed board game?"

"I don't know if I'd called it cursed..."

"I didn't mean to insult," she says. "I was thinking it might fit in well here, if you're looking for some company."

The acrobat's name is Cassio, and in addition to her skilled theatrics she is the co-owner of *The Marvelous Striped Magicians*. Within three months we are kissing while she's suspended upside down, or waiting in the wings, or perched on top of her ledgers. No one will ever be Mina, but I see in her eyes how much she adores me, and she gives me a feeling of stability that I thought I'd lost forever.

Selling games of CurioQueens is better in the tents. We keep a nurse nearby in case of accidents, and there is a big painted board detailing all of the risks and disclaimers. If anything, it only makes our customers more keen. I sleep snuggled in Cassio's wagon every night, and the rest of the troupe are eclectic and friendly.

We only play the game once, Cassio and I, the night we get engaged. She wears me down eventually, saying it's been such a big part of my life, and shouldn't she be included in that, too, before we marry? Which is ridiculous; I only agree because she swears on the whole company that she'll use all the really bad cards on me, if she has to play them, that she'll never use them on herself if she has any other choice.

Afterwards, she threads her arms around my waist and promises there was nothing really bad at all.

"What about moderately bad?" I ask.

"Only tiny bads," she says, and I mostly believe her.

We're married for almost four years. It would have been a lot longer, if it was just up to us, and if two of Cassio's ropes didn't break off their beam while she was thirty feet in the air. There was a thorough investigation that concluded no one human was at fault and ultimately resulted in phrases like "it just shouldn't have happened" and "such terrible luck."

I can't even look at the CurioQueens board after that. I vanish from the troupe overnight and write to my parents in a numb cursive, asking to return home and join the family business, and then promptly set out without waiting for a reply.

In one of the more luxurious neighbourhoods on my way home, I spot an advertisement printed with "*Do you need support for your addiction?*" above illustrations of what are unquestionably CurioQueens cards. If I ever had an addiction to that game I have been thoroughly cured of it by now, but nevertheless I find myself compelled to attend.

The support group is a little over a dozen people, almost all of whom are visibly wealthy, and most of them women. One is gripping an ornate cane like a lifeline. Another sports a flesh-coloured eyepatch and fifteen gem-encrusted rings. Another has a dark veil completely covering her face, with what appear to be diamonds sewn into the bottom hem. Chocolates are served in little metallic parcels, the kind you have to pull the ribbons to unwrap.

I listen to their stories and share the outline of mine, and feel very little besides a vague foolishness and unearned sense of superiority. I only played the game four times in the end, despite it utterly enveloping my life. Fewer than everyone else in this circle, but still three times too many. I roll my wedding rings around in slow, methodical circles. Four times was plenty.

I am one of the first to exit when the session ends, and I'm almost outside when, "Victoria, would you wait, please," reaches me from the other end of the corridor.

I can't remember the speaker's name or any of her stories. She has a long face, too distinctive to be called pretty, but that might be called handsome. As she hurries to catch up to me, she walks with a pinstripe umbrella that matches the pattern on her navy vest.

"I thought you may like to play with me sometime," she says.

I feel my eyebrows knit. "I don't do that anymore."

"I know," she says. "But it's one of the vestiges of my misspent youth, you see. That I have to play at least once a year or I'll pass away." Her lips twitch into a tiny smile, and I realize she must be at least fifteen years older than me. It's the kind of smile my late grandmother used to make while saying things like, "I never did get to do that in the end, but I had a good life."

The woman inclines her head back the way we've come. "Most of them in the parlour have released their boards back into the wild where they can't hurt them anymore. Which, good for them, but you can see how that leaves me in a predicament if I don't wish to die. You, on the other hand, have a board that follows you around."

I tuck my sweaty hands into my pockets so I'm less likely to fidget.

"I promise I'd never hurt you," she's saying, "even in the slightest way."

"That's never been the problem," I mutter.

But she catches my words. Her eyes are sharp. She pulls a scrap of parchment from her vest pocket and tucks it into my dress. "You don't care about me," she says quickly, "and I'll die if I don't. And you'll get to play." She winks, but it's slightly pained. "Think about it."

The parchment is still in my dress, pressed against my breast like both a promise and a cyst.

I go home.

RESTORATION

My wife and I go to get scanned every four months; every quark that we're made up of is recorded as a backup. Our physical and mental states at that moment put figuratively on ice.

After the third scan I feel unusually cold. My wife has appeared in front of me, her face swollen and pink like she's been crying for days. "What's wrong?" I ask. She was fine when we got here.

After the second scan I feel chillier than the first. My wife reaches out to me, her hair greyer and half the length it was thirty minutes ago. "What happened?" I ask, and pull her close.

My wife is waiting for me after my first scan. Somehow she looks years older than when we arrived, and the mixture of emotions on her face is too difficult for me to read. She kisses my hand and says my name like a prayer. Says, "This has to be early enough. Early enough to beat it, because there isn't any earlier."

Then she drives me to the hospital, my hand on her knee.

THE MAGIC IN OUR HANDS

BOB

On the girl's first visit, I take a scraping of the skin from her forearm and provide an overview of the entire process, from what I'll do later that day to when she can get her new hands.

By the girl's second visit I've finished analysing her skin cells. We sit in my office, which provides a similar ambience to a doctor's consulting room, with me seated on one side of my desk and the girl and her parents in comfortable chairs opposite. I glance at the girl's digital file to check her name: Mallie.

"Would you like to hear Mallie's resonance results?" I ask the room.

Mallie's mother has been clutching the brochure I gave her that details all the resonance types, although surely she's known them all since primary school. The paper of the brochure has warped slightly with the moisture of her hands. She lays it in her lap and reaches for her husband, and the combination of her hydro magic and his solar magic creates a thin wisp of steam from where their palms connect.

They nod at me to proceed. "Great," I say. "Like most people, Mallie has two resonance options. That's good. She can pick the one she prefers."

More tense nodding from the other side of the table. Mallie is subtly picking at her nails. Her eyes dart around the room at the wooden name plate between us, the informational posters, and the inoffensive harbour painting behind me.

"Her first option..." I pause for a moment to make sure they're ready. "Is botanical."

Mallie's face visibly tightens, like I've just told her she's been diagnosed with a disease. "Not that one," she says.

"Sure," I agree. Not too surprising; botanical has been unpopular with young people for at least the past several years. They seem to associate it with either 60-year-old gardeners or unwashed hippies.

"Your other option..." I double-check my computer screen. "Is mental."

She releases a long sigh. "Okay," she says. She exchanges reassuring smiles with her parents. "Mental. Okay. I can work with that."

"Good," I say, smiling back at them. The mood in my office is a little lighter. "So you'd like to go ahead and get the gloves made? I can take the scans right now."

I escort Mallie into a second room across the hall, where she sticks her arms into a cylindrical scanner up to the elbow. The machine emits a low buzz as it records the exact shape of her anatomy. I take one scan at rest, one with her fingers spread wide, and one with her hands in fists. It's all over in a couple of minutes, so I don't attempt any small talk.

"We're all done," I confirm. "We'll be ready for your next appointment in eight to ten weeks."

Mallie was my last appointment of the day, so I lock up the customer-facing part of the building and duck into the Grow Lab out the back. Against the wall on the counter stand six specialised 3D-printing machines. It'd be most efficient to start each one processing at the same time and do batches of six, but because teenagers' hands can vary wildly in size the skin gloves take different times to process.

Only one of the machines has an emerald green light on the top, meaning its skin gloves have finished building. I extract them carefully and lay them in a clean insulated bag, which always remind me a little of pizza delivery bags. Then I set up the machine to start growing the next set of gloves in the ever-expanding queue, and take the insulated bag out with me into the warehouse-like space that occupies most of the back of the building.

It's mildly frustrating to have to go through the rigmarole of the portal for only one pair of skin gloves, but I don't want to fall behind. While I go through the automatic motions of climbing into and securing my hazmat suit, I think about the chicken parmigiana I'm going to have for dinner that night, about how I need to re-shave my head on the weekend, about buying more chew toys for Rocky. The suit is heavy, particularly around the shoulders where the helmet sits and from where the rest of the suit falls. It's also particularly weighty where it's strapped around my waist, and in the metal casings around my shoes.

I give the visor of the helmet a quick wipe before I enter the airlock. This time I'm the one being scanned and analysed, to make sure there's no-one with magical capability about to enter the portal. There's not, of course. Most people have two magical resonances, and a smaller number have one or three. About one percent, like me, have no resonance at all. Most of the time I don't mind that I've kept my original hands. I like my job. I don't have to talk to my colleagues or supervisor very often, and I get danger pay.

The airlock system pings with approval, and then the door on the far side opens, exposing the black-peacock-blue of the portal. It shimmers and flows, languid, like an otherworldly oil slick spilled right into the air.

I whistle in the fishbowl of my hazmat helmet and step through clutching the insulated bag, like always.

The portal takes me directly inside our 'shark cage', which is a little larger than a double shipping container in size. Thick, creamy fog hangs around the cage like drapes. I can't see beyond it, although occasionally something has gotten close enough that shadows swim through the air. I avoid the sides of the cage.

Inside the cage are a dozen small pillars that come up to my waist, most of them topped with skin gloves in various stages of transformation. I approach one of the empty pillars and remove the fresh pair of gloves from my insulated bag, double-checking the inside of the wrists. Their owner's name is printed there, plus today's date, and which resonance magic their owner has chosen – if they got to choose. This person did, because the skin gloves are also lined in blue, indicating that their insides are lined with chemicals that attract hydro magic instead of an alternative.

There are glove stands on the top of each pillar; two eight-inch long plastic cylinders, with a golf-ball-sized sphere on the end. I gently slide the new skin gloves onto these stands until the sphere is resting carefully inside the palms, with the hollow fingers stretching up into the inter-dimensional air.

I've been warned in no uncertain terms to never linger on this side of the portal, so on my way back I only check a couple of gloves that look like they might be obviously, visibly ready. A pair of solar magic gloves are nicely blackened around the fingertips and are glowing well enough, but they were printed less than two weeks ago; I will leave them a little longer to be safe. I take a pair of botanical gloves back through the portal with me. A tiny sunflower has bloomed next to a fingernail, and strong shoots have laced themselves through the skin on the back of each hand, like thread.

#

MALLIE

I finish high school in late spring, and then in summer I get my new hands attached. The middle-aged bald guy slathers my old hands with numbing cream, and then dips them in some mild acid to take a few layers of skin off, and then there's some more gel and my new hands get pulled over my old ones and wrapped in bandages, especially around my forearms where the new hands finish. I can't take off the bandages or get anything wet for 48 hours while everything settles.

When everyone is pretty sure my hands won't fall off, Mum and Dad drive me over to the HHOMM (Hawthorn House of Mental Magic) and kiss me goodbye outside the gate so I can go in without them, thank God. The house is three storeys and old and my dad said it's beautiful, but what is really beautiful is the man standing in the doorway beaming at me. His name is Zach Sharpner and he is twenty-something and President of the HHOMM. When he's not looking at anyone he seems like an average guy, I guess, but he has this grin that lights up him and everything around him, and when I walk down the path to the HHOMM that first time he's pointing it at me like a spotlight.

Zach Sharpner takes one of my hands carefully in his two bigger ones, so that the magenta crystals embedded in all our hands don't clink together too hard or too loud or jab into any flesh. Then he takes my suitcases and carries them up to my room on the second floor, which is a little small but fine, and gives me a tour of the whole house. There is a big kitchen and huge living room and so many bedrooms and a sizeable attic. I forget everyone else's names immediately, but they all smile at me with what look like genuine smiles.

Zach says I have a few hours to unpack and get comfortable before dinner, which is always at 7:00, and then there's a movie night tonight to welcome me. "We do great things together at the HHOMM," he says at my new bedroom's door. He pronounces 'HHOMM' with a slightly extended hum, like that noise people make sometimes when they're meditating. "We're so stoked to have you, Mallie. I'm sure you'll do great things with us, too."

Everyone is always busy at the HHOMM. From my third day I am added to the house's roster, and most of the less desirable chores are assigned to the newest members – like me. Scrubbing the showers. Scrubbing the toilets. Scrubbing the tiles in the lobby. There is a lot of scrubbing.

I wasn't used to a lot of cleaning, anyway, but now with chunks of crystals jutting out of my hands it's three times as hard. Harder to hold a brush, harder to not injure myself, harder to keep the sharp edges of my crystals from scraping against the glass. None of the other magic types have anything near as cumbersome growing out of them. Zach finds me on my knees in the entranceway with cracked and bleeding hands, and says, "We can sand down those fresh crystals for you in a couple of weeks. They won't get in your way as much, then. But good to get used to them as they are for now, don't you think?"

I buy a large tub of no-name petroleum jelly from the chemist down the street, and slather it all over my hands every night before bed, which helps a little. Then eventually Zach takes my hands in his own and brings out the sander, which is this little device with a buzzing head the size of my thumbnail, and carefully rubs it over all my crystals until they all have smooth edges and are half as tall as they were before. It takes him a solid hour. We don't speak, because the sander is loud, but my heart is thudding. He only nicks my flesh with the sander once, and he dabs some alcohol on it, and it's no big deal. My new, smaller crystals are such a relief I want to cry. I don't cry, though – not until I'm alone in my room.

When we're not doing chores there are meetings (house meetings, and state meetings with other houses of mental magic) and social nights and fundraisers. Sometimes the meetings seem important and worthwhile, and we vote on things and then the things that we vote on happen. Sometimes the meetings drag on until 1:00 or 2:00 AM and people are just debating or lecturing about the ethics of some obscure mental magic or something, but if you try to leave someone will tell you off and question your commitment to the house.

The social events are often something like the movie night they had on my first day. Some people will sit up the front and watch the movie, but then others will drink beer and play poker or chess, and there's sometimes a couple or two in the corners making out. I am not very good at the poker, but I play because I'm expected to. Some of the cards are slightly sticky from the beer. Maybe the others like playing with me because I'm easy to beat.

We host a lot of fundraisers. I thought the fees my parents paid supported the house, but apparently they only cover basic food and board. They don't cover the upkeep of the building, or the drinks at our social events, or the sanders for our crystals. Every couple of weeks there will be a barbecue on our front lawn, or HHOMM will hire a candyfloss machine, and people from around the neighbourhood will line up out the gate to buy from us. I learn how to bounce a sausage on the hot plate of the barbeque to know when it's done. I learn how to turn a stick in the candyfloss to gather it up into a perfect cocoon, and get my HHOMM t-shirt (the same magenta as our crystals) covered in wisps of spun sugar.

Once a month we are expected to do some Outreach Fundraising (or OFR, because the HHOMM loves acronyms), which is my least favourite anything. We go door-knocking or down to a local shopping centre, in teams of two for back-up and accountability, and we engage random people and ask them to give us money. You smile warmly and offer your hand, and most people will grasp that hand because it's polite, and then you send just a little flow of mental magic through your joined fingers to open their minds. Apparently, this is not illegal because we aren't forcing them to do or part with anything; we're just making them a bit more likely to hear us out, to be mildly curious, to be approachable.

One time I say I can't do OFR, and Zach says, "I thought you liked it here, Mallie. Everyone is expected to contribute," and he looks so disgusted and disappointed that he can barely meet my eyes.

"I'm sorry," I say, "I'm just so tired."

He lets this hang in the air for several seconds, and then beckons me towards him. He places a hand across my forehead, and a strong current of warmth flows through me, in through my head and down into my chest, down my arms, down my legs into my toes. It's pure contentment. It's satisfaction. I feel very tired, still, but now I simply feel better about it.

"Go," says Zach, like he's had enough of me.

I go.

I am majoring in psychology at uni because it seems to go well with my mental magic, but I feel like am not learning much about either psychology or mental magic. Psychology at uni is an appetiser of dull brain anatomy with a main course of even more dull maths, and I used to be good at maths until Year 10 or so when it seems I missed something fundamental and then it was Cs forever. The one good thing about uni is that I can go to the Women's Room between classes and sleep in the musty bunk bed with sheets that probably get changed once a semester, and no-one from HHOMM will come in and ask me to do anything.

I keep reminding myself that I want to be able to use my mental magic and psychology to make people feel better. One of my best friends had a breakdown a few weeks before final exams last year and stepped off the tallest building at school. Maybe if I had enough mental magic I could have helped her. But at the HHOMM, any magic seems to be taught on a need-to-know basis, and everything else is something I should already understand (even though they never told me) or a closely guarded house secret. I tried to do some research online a couple of times, but there's not much reputable stuff up there, and there's so much conflicting misinformation that I gave up and went to sleep.

Towards the end of first semester, one of my buses is cancelled and I decide to walk home from uni. It's the middle of the afternoon, sunny. Bright laughter; though the metal bars of the fence beside me are several girls relaxing in the grass. One is reading a book. One appears to be dozing, a straw sunhat shielding her face. One is playing with a delicate lilac flower that has grown from her knuckles, bouncing it back and forth in the mild breeze. Two are kneeling, spinning a column of sunflowers between them, which starts off inches tall and is soon as tall as they are. A house of botanical magic, obviously, but everyone is young and they all have clean hair and faces. One of them waves at me, and I realise with embarrassment that I've slowed to a crawl; I hurry on and leave them to their flowers.

"Zach," I ask with the courage I've gathered between poker games. "I'd like to learn more magic."

He eyes me somewhat judgmentally, like I shouldn't really have said that but now he's sizing me up anyway. "You know we don't just teach anyone off the streets," he tells me. "You've been working hard for us, though. If you took a position of responsibility at HHOMM, you'd learn more magic. You could put your hand up at the next election." He takes the last swig out of his beer bottle, then leans right in so I feel his breath on my ear. "Just between us, I hear Stephanie's probably leaving the state soon. You could run for Deputy Secretary." He pulls back, and then he's wearing that gorgeous spotlight grin. "Think about it."

"I will," I say. As well as the access to secrets, everyone with official roles in the HHOMM gets fewer chores and a small office and an honorarium. I smile back. "Hey, do you ever use any of your mental magic on us? On me?"

He laughs. "What, without you knowing? Rarely. Most of the time, it's easy enough to get people to do what I want." His grin is even larger.

I like Zach, loathe Zach, and want to be Zach in equal measure. And then the Treasurer returns with our replacement beers.

I stand in my bedroom at the HHOMM, with its free postcards and $20 art posters on the walls, and think about everything I've built here. I could run for Deputy Secretary later in the year. I would probably win. Or I could throw my clothes and a few knick-knacks in my suitcases and disappear into the night. Leave my HHOMM t-shirts in the closet and the

HHOMM doona cover on the bed. Leave half the stuff stuck to the walls. I could.

But the polished crystals in my hands glint in the moonlight, and there's just no point in having magic and not knowing how to use it.

BOB

There's a teenage girl in the waiting area when I go to lock up.

"Hello, I'm Mallie." She smiles warmly and jumps up to shake my hand, and I can feel the protrusions of her mental crystals where she grasps my fingers. "We met about a year ago. I know it's late in the day, but I'm hoping you could just answer one question for me, sir. I won't take long."

She does look vaguely familiar. "One question should be fine," I say.

"Is it possible to change to another resonance type? If you already have your magic established, but there was another type you didn't choose – can you switch?"

I glance at the girl's forearms, where her skin gloves have merged seamlessly with her original flesh. "It's possible. It's not done very often, and you'd need hospital surgery, but it's not out of the question."

She nods and shakes my hand again in thanks, and I feel an unusual glow of contentment from helping.

"Good," she says, smiling. "It's good to have options."

I lock up behind her.

ALL THE TIMES I'M TEN

The first time I turned ten was the most important one. Not because my feats in that lifetime were particularly impressive, but because of Morgan.

We grew up down the road from one another, jumping barefoot across boulders in the river and flying kites made from the scraps of our old shirts. Morgan knew and liked me before I was ten, and that made all the difference.

That first time, they plucked me from our home because of my birthmark, which ranks amongst the silliest reasons to select a chosen one. They trained me in combat and battle tactics and leadership. At the time, when I wasn't a child crying alone in his strange new bedroom, I thought I was special. But I had the best mentorship and the best equipment and the best army. Almost anyone in my place could have succeeded.

Once I had driven back the darkness infecting our land, struck down those responsible, and restored a tentative peace, I was a young man. Everyone knew me and thousands wanted to be my wife. But I only wanted Morgan. She had valued me before anyone cared there was a pale wolf smeared across the brown of my ten-year-old leg. Thankfully, she still did.

We married in the winter and lived a comfortable, quiet life together until I passed in my sleep. The last thing I remember of Morgan is her kissing my forehead and saying, "Goodnight, my hound. Good sleep hunting."

When I awoke, I was ten again.

The second time, I was a girl. It was my tenth birthday, even though it was yesterday that Morgan and I were teaching our granddaughter Sloane how to skip stones. The second time, a magical creature imprinted on me while I was out gathering blueberries for my birthday party, and I was expected to raise it into a beast powerful enough to overthrow the corrupt oligarchy. Adults did not use the word "oligarchy" around me; I was ten. I asked about Morgan and Lydia and Sloane, but they did not exist in that world. I overthrew the oligarchy. I hoped the fledgling democracy we instilled in its place was better.

I was ten many, many times. I was boys and girls and royalty and penniless. I was the goddess's chosen and the girl who could speak to angels and the boy who pulled the enchanted sword from amber. I was the lone survivor of a massacre, a plague, an eruption. I was the girl who assassinated the wicked king, the brightest magician of his age, the most gifted enchanted card player, and the silver-tongued diplomat who secured a treaty with the fae. I was the general who drove the monsters underground. I was the seamstress who wove a new ending for the world while she bled onto the straw.

I was very, very tired.

It started to make more sense why I was the chosen one. I learned very quickly because I was often relearning. I had to adjust to holding a sword in a new body, but I understood swordplay. I had to adjust to new methods of magic, but I knew how it felt to wield it. I had several lifetimes of experience at my disposal. I was the serious child or the strange child or the arrogant child. I knew things a normal ten-year-old would never know.

I was the chosen one.

And every time, I asked about Morgan.

It took forty-six lives for me to find her again.

Morgan's grave is underneath a lemon tree in Sloane's backyard. Morgan lived for six years after first-time me. I'm pleased for her. When I knock on Sloane's door, I am a ten-year-old girl in buttercream robes. Sloane opens the door, sees me, sees my bodyguards.

I tell her I am a relative, and to her credit she does not disagree, even though this time I am as pale as my long-buried birthmark and her family has always been darker.

My bodyguards wait outside. I sit at Sloane's kitchen table and listen to her talk about her family. I eat the carrot cake she offers me, and it is sweet and moist. I lick my fingers. I look around the room and am comforted that she appears to have enough wealth to live on and some to spare. She has a husband and one grown child. She sits opposite me with Morgan's eyes and my original nose, and I smile up at her.

"I know you're supposed to kill the gods," says my beautiful granddaughter. "Do you need my help? Can I do something for you?"

"Yes," I say immediately, to both of our surprise. "I am very tired, and I am ten. I would like you to put me to bed with a glass of milk and read me a story."

Sloane settles me into her son's old bed, and I tuck my head under her arm while she reads. The fire is on. She is a good reader, like Morgan used to be.

Tomorrow, I have a pantheon to dismantle, but tonight I am ten, and the world is quiet.

NOWHERE, AUSTRALIA

The first thing to know about Nowhere, Australia is that no-one ever comes here. There are no roads, no paths in or out, no tyre tracks. Only a few established wooden buildings, eighty twenty-somethings, the rural dust beneath our feet in shades of ochre, smoke and caramel. I don't remember any rain ever arriving, either, but from the stretches of sallow grass around us I presume it must fall sometime.

The second thing to know about Nowhere, Australia is that it's a memory desert. None of us have been here forever, but we couldn't tell you where we were beforehand. We struggle to remember anything solid prior to a few weeks ago. There are suggestions of earlier, forgotten times at Nowhere: old hearts carved into paperbark trees, half-filled holes dug beyond the dining room, ninety-six beds with sixteen of them currently empty. There are notches carved into the wooden slats of the bunk bed above mine, but did someone else carve them, or did I? No journals to act as our substitute memories. No newspaper, TV, or radio to track the dates. No paper at all.

That's not technically true, I think, as I walk back from my dinner of chicken soup in the dining room. There is a single, yellowing clipping displayed behind Perspex beside the assembly hall door. It's a three-and-a-half star review of a play I don't remember scripting, published in a national newspaper I do recognise the name of, with a photo of the actors on set on the assembly hall stage.

I skim the play review again. I must have done this several times in the past, but this time the stars or my brain cells align correctly: in order to write this review, a reviewer must have actually seen the play. The play in our assembly hall. There was a reviewer here – a stranger, a visitor – in our assembly hall.

I am momentarily stunned. Have I had this realisation in the past and forgotten? I must not forget this time. If I write another play and we perform it, will another reviewer come? I must start organising this right now. Right this second.

I'm speed walking towards the fancier dorms and my best friend here, Addison, when a group of four men step in to block my path. Their leader is Kane: big white guy, Aussie flag tattoo, self-trimmed hair hidden under a maroon baseball cap.

"Hey," he says. "Come play Pancake Toss with us."

"Sorry, Kane." I'm already looking past them. "Busy right now."

"No," he says, grabbing my forearm. "Come play."

He's grinning at me, but there's something unfamiliar and off-putting underneath. I have perhaps two seconds to make a decision: will I be safer by continuing to try and extract myself, or by relenting? These guys can be obnoxious but they aren't known to be dangerous. They've played this game a few times before, albeit with consenting participants. Kane's hand tightens on my arm.

"Outside the pleb dorms?" I ask, and Kane takes that as agreement.

Everywhere's close in Nowhere. Once we're in position two of the guys strip me down to my bra and underwear – bare skin is supposed to be easier to grip, but really it's an excuse for seeing my big boobs flop when they toss me – while the other two flip a series of coins to see where I'm going to be held. I shiver for a moment, although the air is still warm.

They hoist me into the air: one right ankle, one left ankle, one right shoulder, and one final hand underneath the left side of my skull. I'm not a fan. They'll toss me up from their waist height, as high as they can, and then try to catch me again with the same four hands, only one hand each. If my feet hit the dirt, no big deal. I'm not keen on my head doing so.

The sun has almost disappeared below the horizon. There are a handful of others outside, chatting or wandering around, but no-one seems to think anything concerning is going on. I turn my head to the right, away from the guy cupping it and from our buildings, and promptly freeze. "Is that horse supposed to look like that?"

My voice must have sounded freaked out enough that Kane and his friends take notice: there's a brief flurry of activity and then they're still. Staring at the horse, I presume. Which is staring straight at us from the grass, with much-too-big eyes as luminous as two full moons.

There is something deeply wrong with this horse. The guys' grip has loosened and I manage to extract myself from their hands as subtly as possible, grabbing my clothes and running off while they're still gazing into the twilight.

I find Addison and her bunkmate Taylor in their dorm room.

Taylor is applying a wet cloth to the forehead of a feverish Indian girl who sleeps in the next bunk; I've forgotten her name, but I can't remember anyone here getting sick before.

I lay down the plan: they'll spread the word around and recruit a cast while I devise the new play for us. About seven characters seems like a good number, the kind of cast that would be easily pictured in a newspaper. To be performed as soon as possible. No-one has to be talented, just determined and willing. Taylor squeezes my hand with her dry one.

I'm up early in the morning, but even so there's an unusual crowd around the first silver vat in the dining room. It's empty. The vats are self-cleaning, so we're used to opening them and finding them empty at certain times of the day. Never this close to sunrise, though.

The vats' pipes quickly disappear into the floor, and there's outraged talk of ripping up the tiles or digging up the patch of dirt outside the dining hall that looks like it was dug up once not too long ago. We have no spades. "Are you planning to use spoons?" I ask, trying to sound as calm as possible. "It might be back in commission by lunchtime."

There's continued grumbling, and someone manages to dint the lid of the empty vat with a piece of cutlery, but eventually the crowd disperses to eat breakfast. There are still three full vats. I take a little less porridge than I normally do, to help make sure there's enough for everyone.

Having eaten, I walk half a kilometre from Nowhere and plan the new play by drawing in the dust with a long stick. It doesn't have to be good, I remind myself: it just needs to be a play. It can be the worst play ever, just as long as a stranger sees it.

I sit in the dust, pressing my hands into the sun-warmed ground, and draw with my fingers instead. By early afternoon I've sweated through my t-shirt and have memorised all the characters, key plot points and sequence of scenes. I jog back to the dining hall before I miss our reduced-kilojoule lunch. The first vat is still empty, of course.

Addison and Taylor have done a great job of drumming up interest in the play, and find I have plenty of potential actors to choose from. I spend the afternoon locating the relevant seven, explaining their characters, and making sure they understand when they should meet me in the assembly hall with their 'costumes' tomorrow. We have no special costumes, of course, so the play is a bad contemporary drama. Rehearsals start tomorrow.

Will spends the evening carving "PLAY IN 2 DAYS" into the assembly hall door with a kitchen knife. We are allowing just enough time for a reviewer to get here and no more.

That night, the horse is closer.

"Should we kill it?" asks Kane. It sounds like he wants to; like he would already be doing so if he had easy access to anything that could pass as a weapon.

"That could make things worse," says Addison.

"Or it could make them better!"

It seems like most of us agree that this horse is a harbinger of Bad News, but we're divided in the response to take. While we argue the horse only stands there silently, unmoving, judging us all with round eyes that glow like tractor beams.

The population of Nowhere starts to physically split into two groups: those who want to kill the horse or not. Remarkably, only a single punch is thrown all night. There are tears, snot; someone spits on the ground. Ultimately, the pro-killing group decides to wait one more day.

By sunrise, two of us are missing.

It takes a couple of hours to confirm they're truly gone. Jennifer, a Chinese girl who was the best at juggling our cutlery, and Gavin, a white guy with a ginger bushranger beard. "Were they together?" I ask Addison, who shrugs.

"Not that I knew of," she says, chewing pensively on a hair tie. "Maybe they just made a break for it."

I murmur my half-hearted agreement. We both know this is unlikely: their belongings are still piled around their bunk beds, and how far would they get with no portable water or food storage?

In the dining hall there are a dozen people sharpening wooden stakes with butter knives. They've broken the legs off our dining chairs, so that the chairs' lopsided corpses look like they're bobbing out at sea. I'm not sure if I'm imagining the faint scent of fear in the air. Cheeks are red, sweaty singlets have been discarded over furniture like flags. The bloodlust for the horse is strong.

I take myself to the assembly hall where my cast has gathered. We walk through the story and the order of scenes one, two, three times across the stage. I make sure they memorise the cues to start and end scenes, and the one or two things that need to happen in each. The rest can be badly improvised. "Good, Taylor," I call from the audience pews.

"Will, when Taylor sits down there, that's when you come in and start the scene in your kitchen."

We run the play until we're confident they can recreate something like it tomorrow. Before the sun sets Will cuts a line through the '2' and the 's' on the door and carves a fresh digit, so it now says "PLAY IN 1 DAY".

When night falls I think our entire population might be gathered to greet the horse. It's closer again. They're clutching their pointed stakes, the women and men of Nowhere who have worked through splinters and bleeding hands to try to defend themselves, and they would've swarmed the horse within seconds if it hadn't been for all the other eyes in the darkness, all aimed across the field and hills like parked car headlights. I quickly count at least twenty sets. Small, frightened gasps echo throughout our group.

One cursed horse, we might've been able to kill. But two dozen?

We lock each dorm room overnight and post sentries to watch through the windows, a stake clutched in each of their hands. I don't know what difference this will really make if the horses decide to come for us, but it seems to give some of us a better sense of control.

I drift in and out of sleep, dozing in my jeans and tank top, and wake with the dawn with an acidic stomach and a scratchy throat. The horses have not come. Thick grey clouds have come in their place, heavy and dark like it's barely daytime at all. I suppose Nowhere's finally getting that rain.

In the dim light of the coming storm, Will updates the message on the assembly hall door: "PLAY TODAY".

"Spread the word," I call to everyone as they slowly rise. "No waiting. Play straight after lunch."

"But..." someone says. "Plays are on at night."

"It's called a matinee."

All of Nowhere packs into the hall for the play's premiere, even Priya with her bad fever, propped up on a pew by two of her friends. Even Kane, with a stake clutched in each of his hands. Even Addison, whose glasses vanished this morning and who can't see more than a metre in front of her.

Thunder rips through the air. "Thank you for coming," I announce briefly. No time for ceremony. No reviewers seem to have arrived yet, but we can only hope that they arrive partway through. "Let's begin!"

My makeshift actors do their best, mostly remembering their cues and storylines, projecting their words over the sound of the heavy rain. They look increasingly nervous. Will tugs at his vest. Taylor stares slack-jawed through the windows of the hall where endless horses and cows are lined up shoulder-to-shoulder, surrounding the hall, their eyes like captured lightning through the glass.

"Say your line, Taylor," I call, digging my nails into my palms. With great strain, she manages to tear her eyes away and meet my gaze.

We don't look at the animals.

"Say your line!"

THE CANDLE QUEEN

The Candle Queen must always carry the sacred candles on her head; otherwise the world will end.

They take us for training when we are eight years old. Old enough that a child probably won't cry immediately when separated from its parents, and may not ever cry, ever at all.

We are picked for our self-control and stamina. The only two qualities needed. The only two qualities they ever test us on. If I had understood this earlier, I might have misbehaved in order to avoid selection, although it would have been a struggle as I am competitive by nature. We sleep in a long room with twenty-six beds. Twenty-six beds for twenty-six girls. They give us new names, one for every letter of the alphabet.

Our training ends when we are seventeen. They pick me, out of twenty-six girls, because the testing has proved me the best. "The Candle Queen," they say, "our unflinching rod. She who could stand in the flames and not scream."

They bring me to the Underground Palace. The current reigning Candle Queen is there. She is sixty-seven. She has served her purpose. They lift the Candle Crown from her elderly neck and place it onto mine, a rounded metal bowl to fit over my head with a circular silver plate on top and a strap to secure it under my chin. Three large candles sit on the plate, and it is heavy, but this is what I have trained for.

They sew me into the dress I will wear for the next fifty years, and there is singing that fills the chamber like bells.

I spend my days being vigilant. I make no decisions, and I am responsible for nothing except holding up the candles. If one goes out or burns low, someone in my entourage will immediately replace it with the next candle in the series. But I must keep my head straight and my concentration unwavering, for if all three go out this will trigger the end of the world.

My days follow a strict routine. When I wake, I am cleaned by my handmaidens, who wash me and replace my underclothes, and I eat the breakfast that is chosen for me.

I have my morning walk, in the same corridors each day where the sacred wax has hardened into hills on the stones. I wear my slippers with the thin rubber soles in order to feel each lump of fallen wax with my feet. I eat an early lunch. In the afternoon, someone will come and read to me or play for me, or I will meditate. I have my evening walk before dinner. After dinner, the masseuse comes to work on my neck and shoulders, and the handmaidens return to wash me once again. Lastly I am put to bed, which requires three different pieces of machinery so that I may sleep with the candles burning above my skull.

After many months of this constant order I come to understand the magnitude of something changing. And it is only a small thing, but when I am eighteen, something does.

My evening wash is slower. My handmaidens always come in pairs, one to watch the candles while the other cleans, and they usually wipe me like a precious vase. Tonight the cloths are gentler, still careful and precise, but there is an added tenderness now, too. I am reminded of when my mother used to bathe me as a small child. Those are unhelpful thoughts, so I focus on the warm cloth as it tucks itself between my toes, over my creases, around the backs of my knees. The handmaiden's breath on my cleansed thighs. The salve she applies around my hips where the seams of the mesh dress rub against my skin.

When she slides out from my skirt and packs up her materials, I ask, "What is your name?"

She jolts a little as she stands. She is petite, like all of the handmaidens, so they can fit beneath my dress, and her eyes are too big for her face. She glances at me furtively, like she is trying to deduce if I am angry. She says her name is Anne.

"Anne!" I announce, loud enough to get the attention of the guard by the door. "I like Anne. Bring me more Anne."

He nods, and it is done.

The next morning, Anne is wiping my jawline as she would paint a canvas. A fleck of blue wax is buried in a fingernail of her free hand. Eventually she notices the target of my gaze, flicks the wax from her nail and colours slightly.

"Have you ever seen the sacred wells, my queen?"

"I have not."

"They took us there as part of our training," she says, tucking the soft cloth behind my ear. "My favourite was the blue. It's in a landlocked part of the country, but right around the well, it smells so strongly of the sea. If you close your eyes, the breeze passes over the wax and across your cheeks, and it's like you're at the ocean after all."

She smiles hesitantly, as if checking for my approval.

I place my hand on to hers, only for a moment. "You can tell me."

She continues, "Every day, we give thanks that the sacred wax continues flowing to the surface, carrying the magic from our earth's core. We meditate on it in our daily circles, and if I concentrate hard enough on the blue wax, I'm not just underground anymore, I'm taking the sandy path towards the ocean near my childhood home. I can hear the lull between each wave, and everyone I pass greets me by name, and I'm all warm from their cheer and from the sun flickering off the water. Or I'm chasing crabs and treasures across the rockpools with my cousins, and we're laughing and trying to stay out as late as possible, before the tide or nightfall takes us home."

We agree that she will return in the afternoon to describe the rest.

So Anne perches in the fragile wooden chair in the corner and regales me with stories of the green well, where the wax seems to grow across the clearing like vines, and the yellow well, where she had to wear a tightly knotted veil to stop its brightness blinding her. At the pink well, the semi-liquid wax moulded itself into mouths and howled as it was harvested. The red well bubbled like an overflowing saucepan, and the orange well grew a solid crust in seconds no matter how the wax was heated, so harvesters constantly broke the top with pickaxes.

When she has finished she bends over my skirt to kiss me on the back of my wrist, and as she does she presses something wriggling into my palm. It stills when I close my hand over it, smooth and waxy; familiar. I try to slow my heartbeat, reserving my judgement for when I can examine it properly.

Later, in the eternal candlelight of my sleeping hours, I open my stiff fist to see a tiny wax elephant unfurl its trunk. It wobbles its head, which billows its ears like sails, and then it runs up my arm to settle on my shoulder. I turn my head towards it with practised steadiness; its blue wax body smells of salt, and seaweed, and something new and clean; what I imagine the ocean would smell like.

Unlawful, I think, *sacrilegious*, and see those words like black wax falling into water. Our sacred wax should never be used for something so frivolous, and certainly not by a handmaiden, who is forbidden from crafting with the wax at all. I feel a queasiness, I think, a churning in my stomach. The little elephant trumpets up at me from my scapula, but it makes no sound.

Anne comes to administer to me the following night. Her demeanour reminds me vaguely of my childhood dog after puncturing a pillow or coating something forbidden in its salt-and-pepper hair. Mother and father always thought that it looked guilty, but I knew that look was fear. The extremities of Anne's hands are shaking, ever so slightly.

She kneels before my skirt on the waxy black stones, avoiding my eyes. She pulls her tools from the white pouch around her hips and sets them beside her on the floor.

"Anne," I say. "I'm glad to see you."

Some of the tension in her shoulders drops away. "My queen."

I correct her gently, sharing with her the name I was given at eight.

She repeats it, still not meeting my gaze, and ducks under the rim of my skirt to kiss my feet. There is a small shower of kisses, somewhere between a thank-you and apology, and improper regardless. Then she sets to work cleaning her lips off my skin.

She seems to calm and grow in confidence as she wipes her way up my legs. Before too long I feel a slow, deliberate kiss on the back of my left knee. "I hope I am not hurting you today, my queen," Anne says quietly. "Is this okay?"

"Yes," I say.

Her warm breath spirals higher up my leg, stopping just before the crease that separates my thigh from my hips. "And this, my queen?"

I press my thumbnail into the pad of my forefinger, just enough to feel it. "Yes."

Anne replaces her breath with the heat of her mouth. And then her breath is moving sideways, to where she has two fingers hooked into my underclothes. "Is this okay?" she says.

And I say yes.

No-one in the room notices anything out of the ordinary; not the handmaiden with her eyes affixed to the candles on my head, not the guard rigid by the door. On the outside, I am the unflinching rod, the only thing I was ever trained for.

Inside, I am melting honeycomb, running all the way down.

The little blue elephant stops moving on the fifth day.

"Have you ever thought," Anne speaks so low into the shell of my ear, "of living somewhere else?"

"No," I say. "I have my duty."

She drags the cool salve across the latest wax burns on my arms. I can see her furrowed brow from the corner of my eye and feel the ghost of a long-forgotten urge to smirk.

Instead, I say, "Do you not believe that the world would end if not for me?"

"I believe it." She leans into me again, her chest pressing against the waxy crust of my shoulder. "I just don't believe it has to be you."

#

In the end, I am not convinced until it happens.

On the night in question, Anne treads in for my evening wash. Firstly, she offers the guard the same beverage she has been bringing them for weeks, although tonight when he sips it, his eyes glass over and his face slackens. Earlier, she convinced the handmaiden rostered alongside her of a mix-up, and she is accompanied by a girl I have only seen before in mirrors. I take its hand; waxy and smooth. A perfect likeness of me shaped out of wax, one that Anne has spent months crafting and then breathed temporary life into, in the way she has been practising for years.

"Undress," she tells my wax doppelganger, and it does, while Anne takes a pair of nail scissors from her utility pocket and cuts the line of stitches at the back of my dress. The weight of it shifts over me like a cocoon breaking. I want to gasp at the feeling of the air across my spine. Instead, I stare at the guard by the door, but he is studying the painting on the opposite wall of our country's wax-red poppies.

"I told you not to worry," says Anne over my shoulder. "As long as all the flames stay lit and no-one screams, we are beneath his notice."

I steady myself with a couple of deep breaths and bend my knees until the hem of the dress is touching the floor. Then, with Anne's help, I slowly extract myself backwards from the dress's shell, making sure my head stays ramrod-straight as always.

I am out. My bare skin feels baby-new. I fear I will choke on my adrenaline.

Anne reaches out for the strap that keeps the candles on my head. I grab her arms. I would cry, I think, if I was still capable. "How do we know?"

She tells me: "There will still be a Candle Queen who will stay vigilant, and make no decisions, and follow orders and keep her concern solely for the candles on her head, because I tell her to. And when she stills they will find another, perhaps your second-best alphabet sister, and she will carry the candles until she decides otherwise." Anne's eyes glow brighter than any wick. "Don't you want to try?"

When we finally lift the metal bowl from my scalp, it feels like cutting the umbilical cord between my body and the world.

We leave the wax queen sitting in my sleeping apparatus. Anne has tucked my matted mess of hair under a white handmaiden's cap, and we pass the guard that way, one regular-sized handmaiden and one overgrown.

We keep walking. We walk all the way outside, the backs of our hands brushing. I feel so light I may just float off into the sky.

Has the world ended? It might, I know.

But not yet.

SOLACE

It started with scissors.

Cora van Ellison had been working ten-hour days, hurrying to get several commissions ready and putting the final touches on her end-of-year collection. She was clumsy at the best of times, and then she dropped some scissors and successfully caught them; then wished she hadn't because of the surprisingly deep gouge in her left palm that needed stitches.

Two days later: a busy day of travelling between the generation ship's connecting pods. She had two meetings in the Verdant pod that morning, predominantly to confirm that her clothes sat correctly around their prehensile tails. After lunch, she ventured thirty kilometres across the ship into Blue Skies, where the residents were all fifty percent taller than anyone else on the ship, and where she needed to climb a ladder for most measurements. And lastly, there was Solace, to design for Meadow Fullstone.

The appointment was for 16:30, when anywhere else on the ship would have been bathed in artificial sunlight, but Solace was dark. Meadow was wealthier than most of her pod-mates, and her house boasted two full stories above ground. Lights in the shapes of dragonflies, tigers, and hummingbirds welcomed Cora to her front door. Meadow greeted Cora with a kiss on each cheek and some cherry-flavoured tea.

The first half of the appointment elapsed normally, even if Cora thought she saw something unsettling from the corner of her eye. Then there was something skittering near her feet and she flinched automatically, enough to stick Meadow's soft skin with a sewing needle and draw blood. Enough to open up the wound on Cora's own left hand, which she'd left uncovered for ease of use, and then she felt so mortified that she fumbled with the needle and managed to mix that tiniest smear of Meadow's blood with her own.

It had been stupid, as many life-changing events often are.

Once Cora had apologised profusely, she raced into the bathroom, initially to press a wad of tissue paper to her bleeding hand, but then to vomit into the cold toilet bowl. She emerged dizzy and shaking, and Meadow pressed a hand against her forehead and said, "Oh dear, oh dear," again and again, and insisted that Cora stay the night as she was in no condition to go anywhere.

Recovery took a few days. Meadow or her housekeeper brought a variety of soups morning, noon, and night, often made with the leafy greens, carrots and herbs that thrived in Meadow's garden. They fed Cora vitamin D pills, and Meadow read to her from a favourite novel about a ship that sailed across oceans instead of space. As Cora became more lucid, she came to understand what had happened to her. The new skin around her wound was growing back milky-white. Meadow felt deeply guilty and promised she'd pay for Cora to be cured, but as it required a hospital stay, there was a six-month wait; Cora could stay in Meadow's backyard studio until then.

Almost everyone who lived in Solace had a severe genetic allergy to the ship's lights. It had been introduced to the Solace pod about fifty years ago: blood-transmissible and gene-altering. Many spoke of bio-terrorism. There had been rumours that Admin themselves were responsible, but only rumours. Eventually, it had become such a normal part of life that its origins were rarely mentioned at all.

The first couple of weeks were the worst. Cora's collection never walked the runway. Her commissions were late: she contacted her clients and apologised; she was very sick. Some days it seemed pointless to leave the bed; perhaps she could hibernate for the next six months until her hospital appointment. Occasionally communications from extended family or friends arrived, but replying felt impossible. Despondent, she sunk into the grass in Meadow's back garden and marvelled that those flowers and plants could still grow when Solace was only bright between 22:00 and 5:00 hours.

Meadow took her hand and taught her their names: deadnettle, rhapis palm, bromeliads, birds nest fern, caladium, devil's ivy. The caladiums were Cora's favourite, with their heart-shaped leaves and variegated colouring, each leaf green around the outside and a bright pink in the middle.

One evening, staring down at her artificial steak, she asked, "Why don't you get the cure as well? Why doesn't everyone in Solace?"

Meadow chuckled. "Well, the cure is expensive, and it takes time. But mostly, people here are quite happy with their lives." She squeezed Cora's fingers for reassurance. "Let's say you grew up somewhere where everyone had wings. Almost nothing is at ground level. All of the building entrances are at least three metres up with no ramps or stairs or built-in ladders. You would be disabled in that society, wouldn't you? It wasn't built for you."

She gestured to the darkness outside her window, to the roses thriving under special garden lights. "Solace is just about perfect for us."

Meadow had dimples when she smiled, Cora realised. The heaviness of the recent weeks slowly began to lift.

Soon after, Meadow took her to the bustling Dark Market, which shone with a hundred types of lights and where children revelled with lit-up balloon animals and glowing face paint. Adults were mostly draped in black, or they wore illuminated clothing where the fabric pulsed or changed colour with the music or temperature. "You could design outfits better than this," Meadow said into her ear, as they bought chicken-salted popcorn and flaming cocktails you blew out like birthday cake.

They attended a Gothic cabaret bar, where Meadow knew the owner and smuggled Cora backstage to sing songs with the cast after the show. Cora sang quietly, embarrassed that she only knew the choruses and could barely hold a tune, but no one seemed to mind. While Meadow held court with the performers, the pianist painted Cora's makeup to better flatter her new complexion.

The next week, at a liquid meat tasting, Cora interrogated Meadow on the realities and dangers of their condition.

"Well," said Meadow, wiping a drop of pseudo-shark off her lip. "Direct exposure to the ship's lights will leave your skin blistered quickly. If it continues, then comes the fever, and that leads to unconsciousness within about fifteen minutes. And yes, people can die from it..." She deliberately caught Cora's eyes. "But that happens so rarely these days; I can't remember the last time someone died from allergic light exposure."

"And going outside the pod?"

"It's doable," Meadow said. "A lot of clothing here, like what I commissioned from you, is long and dark and draped. If I were leaving Solace, I would add thick stockings, long gloves, a full hood that covered my neck and shoulders. They come with translucent fabric across the eyes, and then you wear goggles underneath." She swirled her glass and sighed. "It's a lot. It can be hot, and some people look at you strangely. But it's done." A pause. "Or there's always the Solace version of a bodysuit."

When Cora was measuring her Solace time in months instead of weeks, Meadow took her to some underground baths modelled after ancient hot springs. Meadow, like many of its patrons, bathed nude, and her figure was stunning. Cora blushed at being caught staring as water dripped down Meadow's body through the steam, and quickly muttered something about wanting to make more dresses for her. Meadow seemed predominantly amused, wading to sit two hands' lengths away; Cora thought she could have kissed her then, if it hadn't been so early and things hadn't felt so unequal, and if Cora had been more sure of what she wanted.

She'd been serious about the dresses. She sewed Meadow long dresses and short ones, dresses with queenly collars and dresses with bat-wing sleeves that hung between the wrists and waist. Above-the-knee ruffled skirts that could be untied for floor-length light protection, and tops with a huge hidden hood that could billow around the wearer like a parachute. Jumpsuits with tiny lights sewn into them like embroidery. A long, silky gown with arms that finished in its own gloves, that covered everything except Meadow's face and came with a fabric crown seamlessly built to the garment at the top of the head.

Cora designed for Meadow, and for Meadow's friends, and then for Solace. Over time, Cora had her things gradually transported from her old apartment into the backyard studio, which was still hers even though she sometimes slept in Meadow's enormous bed. She made clothes for Solace, and she tended the garden.

Finally, while Cora and Meadow sat beside the caladiums with fresh mugs of cherry tea, Cora asked, "How would you feel if I cancelled the hospital appointment?"

Meadow didn't look at her. Very evenly, she said, "Does that mean you would stay here? Stay with me?"

"If I could."

"Well," Meadow said, reaching for the hand Cora injured with scissors months ago. "That would be glorious."

LAST TEXT

Mikala Godfrey receives the final texts that people send before they're murdered.

She has a shrine for this in her house; a smartphone on a stand, from where she copies the texts into a series of identical leather notebooks. She calls this 'keeping witness.' She kneels before the phone every day in a strapless black dress, resting on a gel pad to help save her knees. We tried taking her phone away once, but the texts only switched to arriving on Mikala's replacement phone. They want her to see them.

Most of them follow the same pattern: *I love you. I'm so scared. I don't want to die. I think he's coming.* But she also gets the ones where they obviously have no idea. Where they say they just put the washing on, or isn't this episode great, or just *k*.

We visit her regularly, me and my partner Steve. We sit in what she calls her "Greeting Room" with the glass coffee table and the couches that are a little too hard to be comfortable. We ask about murders, and she finds the relevant ones in her notebooks (if they can be found), and we photograph the transcription. Some of them aren't relevant at all; she receives all of the texts-before-murder written in English, from all around the world, and since she started learning French she receives some in French as well. She says she'll learn German next.

Sometimes we sit there for a while, so I start to bring cookies in a bag. Then danishes. Then petit fours. Mikala serves us water, coffee, a pitcher of homemade iced tea. She starts to ask for a trade before she slides over the transcripts: a description of our breakfasts this morning, or a ballpoint pen, or the top button of my shirt. All small enough that we don't protest about handing them over. A stone lodged in the tread of my shoe. The weather forecast for tomorrow. A kiss.

We are not in a relationship, Mikala and I. We have never exchanged phone numbers nor made any effort to meet outside her home. Still, that doesn't stop her from asking me to draw a rabbit and a bee in Sharpie on her upper arm. She has them tattooed there permanently. It doesn't stop me from thinking of her when I'm alone, and my hand dips beneath the sheets.

At the last minute, Steve says – unconvincingly – that he is sick and I should go and see Mikala alone. She takes me through the white door to her shrine, and I see that she has updated the stand and gel mat to a little desk and an ergonomic chair that still has her half-kneeling. Very sensible. Near the desk with the smartphone is what looks like a small altar. There is my pen, my button, the stone... But she has retracted into herself. I would distract her from her important work, she says.

I start to bring fewer pastries, less often. Mikala stops asking for trades for the transcripts. Steve and I are sent into the bush for a rural investigation, and when I put my officer's hat back on it seems to be vibrating, and then there's a sharp sting on the top of my scalp.

The bee or wasp flies away. My head burns and balloons, but I was stung as a kid with no real consequences, so I tell Steve I'm fine. Within minutes, though, I'm itchy. Getting dizzy. My throat has closed up, and I feel like I could vomit if its passage wasn't blocked by the swelling. Steve calls an ambulance, but out here I know they won't reach us in time.

Acutely struggling to breathe, I retrieve my phone and text my own number. I tell Mikala that I love her, that she was the greatest thing in my whole life. When I hit send, my own phone beeps a moment later.

Then I'm lying in the dirt. I'm gasping, my own gun pressed against my temple. Steve's pleading with me, saying that he can pass the message on, that we don't have to do things this way. But I want to. The edges of my vision are receding. I wrap his hand around my own, with the gun underneath them both. "Please," I manage to get out, although now my tongue is swollen, too. "Please."

Steve pulls the trigger.

Mikala gets a text.

LA VIE EN MER

Episode notes

Season 1

1.1 SAIL AWAY

As our global future spirals into more danger and chaos, *La Vie En Mer*, a luxury cruise ship with 500 occupied residential apartments, is still sailing. Fearing our earth is becoming uninhabitable, a team of four scientists (Grace, Cara, Kenji and Jackson) who live onboard create a device that can propel *La Vie En Mer* into an unlimited number of parallel earths, hoping to find a new perfect world for them to call home. The first parallel earth they visit is one where dinosaurs and megafauna never went extinct.

1.2 THE VOTE

Back on our earth, the population of *La Vie En Mer* is scandalised that their ship was transported into a parallel universe without their knowledge or consent. The scientists apologise; they explain that they had only intended to run tests and were truly surprised when their work was successful. A vote is held: 72% of the ship votes to continue to travel to more parallel worlds, so long as appropriate safety protocols are devised and followed. Sixteen people choose to permanently disembark at the nearest port; they watch from the shore as *La Vie En Mer* prepares to deliberately travel to a new parallel world for the first time.

1.3 DAYBROKEN

The ship arrives in a world that initially seems abandoned, although there is evidence of recent human civilisation. It soon becomes clear that the human population of this world only emerges on the surface at night, as it's considered too dangerous to live in the daylight. While some of the ship's passengers, like Grace and Jackson, are deeply curious to investigate the validity of and reason behind this, many more frightened passengers simply want to move on. Grace and Jackson must race back to the ship so that they're not left behind at daybreak.

1.4 TURBULENT WATERS

Disconnected from their usual reality, the residents and crew of *La Vie En Mer* have stopped receiving their regular pay packets, and increasingly urgent questions arise about how money should function in the small-town ecosystem of the ship. Why should the crew continue to work hard when the residents aren't working at all? As they sail across a world that's almost entirely underwater, there is plenty of time for everyone to argue, strike, and ultimately, reach a tentative peace with one another. Many of the residents begin to work in some fashion, either by training in certain roles like food preparation or cleaning, or by contributing with their expertise in other ways. Cara teaches a popular introductory science class; Kenji reluctantly opens up an electronics repair service.

1.5 YOUR FACE

The ship docks somewhere extremely similar to its original world, complete with all the accompanying destruction and mess. Jackson double-checks the coordinates to ensure they haven't returned home. On land, Grace meets a version of her dead husband who is still alive, but he doesn't recognise her. She pleads with him to join her aboard the ship, but then slowly realises that this parallel version of him is very different to the man she married.

1.6 TIPPING POINT

Immediately after arriving on a new world, the occupants of *La Vie En Mer* are alarmed to find their ship resting on sand rather than sea, and the ship starts to tip on its hull for a few seconds before it can be transported back to the previous world. Although the furnishings on board are designed to cope with strong waves, there is still some property and bodily damage, and the medical bay grows full to bursting. Grace mourns her broken violin. Kenji's eleven-year-old daughter has a concussion. The scientists work with the crew to bolster safety protocols, but some passengers won't be calmed. The ship takes a brief detour to its home world to drop off twenty passengers who are too terrified to continue travelling to new worlds.

#

1.7 FUEL

The scientists cautiously explore a world where humans have been superseded by androids. Jackson, a widower, flirts with an android with detachable deer antlers, and in return for becoming her live test subject in a few low-risk experiments, she upgrades the ship's engines so that they run super-efficiently on sun and wind power, essentially providing a lifetime of fuel. Afterwards, Jackson asks her to stay on the ship, and she admits that while she's tempted by the adventure, their relationship would be far too intellectually unequal. Meanwhile, Kenji considers permanently leaving to live with the androids, but decides against it when his family would be disembarking with little more than the clothes on their backs.

1.8 SEA DAY

Overwhelmed by recent events and bolstered by the new fuel upgrade, *La Vie En Mer* takes a quiet 'sea day' and temporarily postpones travelling to the next world. Cara swims laps in the pool and then slow dances with her husband. Grace struggles to relax and alternates between drinking cocktails and tending the hydroponic garden. Kenji enjoys some family time on the sun deck, watching his twins play table tennis or read to their parents from the play they're writing. Jackson fishes off his balcony with his daughter, catching otherworldly species of fish they've never seen before. After dinner, the four scientists reconvene to play a competitive game of Settlers of Catan.

1.9 RESCUE PARTY

Shortly after disembarking in a frigid new world, a group of passengers including Kenji and Jackson are kidnapped by the locals and spirited away into the mountains. Following a failed attempt at diplomacy, Grace and Cara must rally, organise, and arm a rescue party; they construct a makeshift flamethrower and a stock of other homemade weapons. While the rescue party is successful, one of the ship's residents dies and Jackson loses his right foot.

1.10 UTOPIA

La Vie En Mer finally arrives at a world that seems promising – and it only gets better and better. While it's less technologically advanced than their home world the environment is healthy, the culture is pleasant, and the locals are hospitable; they even fit Jackson with a prosthetic foot without wanting anything in return. The ship is ready to set down permanent anchor when Grace spots an earth-shattering meteor in the sky.

Season 2

2.1 FRESH MEAT (PART 1)

The population of *La Vie En Mer* argues over where to house the dozen refugees they were able to save from the meteor world. Without extended back and forth, it's agreed that any empty residential suites will be filled by the more senior members of the crew, and that the refugees can then live in the less luxurious ex-crew accommodation. As the refugees struggle to settle in, one night the pool isn't drained as normal, and the next morning a dead body is found floating there.

2.2 FRESH MEAT (PART 2)

Investigations continue into the dead body, identified as Frank, a seventy-ish retired mining manager. His wife says he left their suite about 2:00 AM and never came back. Eventually, as the autopsy shows no signs of foul play, there are no witnesses, and no-one seems to have any clear motive for killing Frank, his death is ruled an accident. Attentions then turn to who was responsible for leaving the pool full overnight, and whether this warrants banishment from the ship. Ultimately it is decided that they won't be banished for this first offence. However, in the course of investigations it was uncovered that another passenger had been beating his wife and child: this, instead, triggers the first banishment.

2.3 EVOLUTIONS

La Vie En Mer arrives in a world where humanity has diverged into several different species, aided by a mix of genetic engineering and other technologies. At first, the ship's passengers are entranced by the winged, hollow-boned species; the scaled species with gills and bio-luminescent patterns; the super-tough species that can survive deep in the sea or high in the air or even inside a volcano, where other humans would perish. Later, a sub-set of the ship's population would still like to set down permanent anchor, but many more consider this a dangerous place for them, and that living here would make them feel weak and useless.

#

2.4 HUNGER MAKES ME (A LONELY GIRL)

Jackson's nine-year-old daughter, Nia, confides to Grace that she kept a strange fish they caught on Sea Day in a tank, but it died, and then she cooked it in a microwave and ate it. Ever since then, she's been experiencing strong urges for human flesh. Despite Grace's alarm, she calms Nia down and runs some tests, and then fetches her some antibiotics from the medical bay. Grace promises a crying Nia that she won't tell anyone unless the antibiotics don't work and things get worse. Nia confesses that she killed Frank by accident: she'd gone for a cookie, but Frank's ankle was just standing there, looking delicious, and biting it gave him a terrible fright.

2.5 A WORLD OF THEIR OWN

The ship discovers a world where men haven't existed for 100 years and all remaining humans are female. Although these women are cautiously interested in exchanging technology, food, and other culture with *La Vie En Mer*'s passengers, most of them will only speak with other women. Cara quickly makes new friends and networks, but then must leave them as staying wouldn't seem fair to her husband. Jackson experiences a mix of emotions attempting to woo the locals; those who find him interesting view him as a novelty.

2.6 STOWAWAY

Grace's search for a horticultural tool leads her into the ship's deep storage, where she discovers an almost-mermaid who has hidden away since they left the world with divergent human species. Much of her small body is scaled, and her legs are attached together with a web of thick skin to aid with swimming. After bringing her supplies for a couple of days, the two bond and Grace smuggles her upstairs to live in the bath in her suite.

2.7 RUN AGROUND

The ship materialises in a universe where Earth doesn't exist and where its deck is suspended in the unforgiving cold of outer space. Kenji and Jackson frantically propel *La Vie En Mer* into a second parallel universe; it only takes a few seconds, but afterwards, they are out of commission in the medical bay. The other passengers soon discover that the air of this new world is poisonous, but they can't easily escape again as the device that allows them to travel to parallel worlds has broken. As the residents seal the indoors of the ship with towels and duct tape, Cara and Grace must work together to bring the broken device back to life.

#

2.8 ORGANS

The health of Cara's husband, Daniel, is obviously deteriorating, and the ship's medical team suspect he has a rare form of cancer. Cara implores Grace, Kenji and Jackson to take *La Vie En Mer* back to the world of androids, believing they can fix him. While her friends are sympathetic, they say they can't steer the ship based on the needs of just one or two people. Eventually, they agree to take a brief detour to the android world, just long enough for Cara and Daniel to jump into a lifeboat. Once on land, Cara negotiates for Daniel to be fixed in return for surrendering several of their human organs.

2.9 THE ONES WHO SAIL AWAY...

La Vie En Mer arrives at another world that seems almost too perfect. It comes at a price: at the heart of each city lives one child who is intentionally horribly neglected, starving and alone in a tower cell. Grace and Jackson reluctantly go to view one of these children and immediately realise that the child is a hologram. They are riddled with indecision; if they say something and break the spell of the citizens' belief, will that somehow ruin the utopia? At the same time, the other passengers of *La Vie En Mer* don't know about the hologram, and many of them can't morally reconcile living there. Eventually, the ship simply sails away.

2.10 EXPECTATIONS

The ship takes a brief detour to pick up Cara and Daniel, who now have several new synthetic replacement body parts between them. *La Vie En Mer* then docks at a world where they are immediately greeted as gods. The locals are delighted by the passengers' advanced technology and knowledge, and they shower their guests with feasts, festivities, and attention. However, relationships quickly sour when the locals make demands that the passengers can't fulfil, and when they try to bottle pieces of the passengers that won't magically regrow. The almost-mermaid liberates Grace when she's held underwater to harvest her breath, and Cara is saved by her new metal heart that can't be easily pierced.

#

Season 3

3.1 TWINS

Grace introduces the scientists to the almost-mermaid, Ostari, who has been living in her suite. They are dating now. The ship sails across a world where almost all the life appears to have died out. In the remains of his hometown, Kenji discovers green-tinted versions of his twins who survived the apocalypse. Before he died, their version of Kenji gave them the ability to consume most of their energy via photosynthesis. As these twins seem strange but inherently good-hearted, he brings them back to the ship to meet his other children, and their family expands to six.

3.2 HOME INVASION

In the next world, *La Vie En Mer* is immediately boarded by pirates. The passengers panic as they can't escape by shifting worlds; the pirates come with them. Everyone must band together to fight back, either by killing the pirates or throwing them overboard. The lower decks are locked down as much as possible, and most elevators are stopped. Cara unearths the makeshift flamethrower. Jackson uses the bars' bottles as bludgeoning weapons and projectiles. Grace stalks the pirates who have made it to the residential hallways, injecting them with incapacitating drugs. Kenji and his wife engineer some spears and commandeer a motorised luggage cart. At the end of the day, all two dozen pirates are dead, plus thirty-three passengers, including Daniel.

3.3 VEILS

La Vie En Mer is in mourning. After two weeks of funerals, repairs, medical care and recovery post-pirate-attack, the restless population votes that it's time to keep moving on. The ship arrives at a bustling market where everyone wears masks. Cara, deeply grieving her husband, drifts off the ship, puts on a fox mask and disappears into the crowd. Her friends' concern increases exponentially when they see the locals sleeping in their masks, showering in their masks, carrying babies that wear masks. They hurry to find Cara and pry the mask from her bloody skin, where it's already partially merged with her face.

3.4 ANCESTRY

The ship docks in a world where each of the locals consult an AI several times a day. Whenever anyone needs to decide on anything more significant than dinner, they touch a shimmering silver surface and the AI gives them the answer. The locals explain that before anyone dies, their intelligence and memories are added to the AI, so that the wisdom of their collective ancestry is always at their fingertips. Grace, Jackson and Kenji hurry back to the ship before the AI can tell anyone they're a threat – or that their brains would be useful to add to the trove. Cara has stayed on board, and when the other scientists return, she says she's done looking for new worlds: everyone should vote on a world for the ship to return to permanently, and if anyone's unhappy with the result they can be dropped off beforehand at another world of their choice.

3.5 ENDLESS

La Vie En Mer explores a world of immortal humans and their equally immortal pets. Everyone is thriving on a beautiful earth, with one catch: in order to prevent overpopulation, having any new children is forbidden. This sparks a furious debate aboard *La Vie En Mer*, including between our scientists: Grace and Cara are happy to exchange the unlikely possibility of future children for immortality. Jackson and Kenji both want their kids to have kids of their own, and Jackson wants more children himself if he can find the right woman. The numbers are close. When the ship sails on, it's with Grace and Cara openly campaigning for a vote to choose a previous world to permanently return to.

3.6 ALL THE FLAVOURS

The ship materialises in a world that humans share, mostly harmoniously, with multiple alien races. *As La Vie En Mer*'s passengers wander around in awe, one of the aliens takes a swift liking to Jackson. Despite her being half his size with purple skin, four catlike eyes and a winglike membrane like a sugar glider, he quickly likes her, too. Regardless of their connection, she refuses to leave her home for his ship. Knowing that the ship is likely to choose a permanent home soon, he promises to come back to her. He is now all-in on the vote to choose a permanent residence from the worlds they've visited previously.

3.7 EXTRA LARGE PINK RETRIEVERS

La Vie En Mer discovers a world where fantastic, genetically engineered pets (and humans) are a worldwide craze. Kenji's children fall in love with the animals there, particularly a giant, pink-coloured golden retriever that they can ride. As there is nothing significantly wrong with this world, Kenji is keen to stay there for his family. Under any other circumstances the ship's passengers would've probably voted to stay there, but now they're aware that they can vote for somewhere they'd personally like better. The date for that final vote is set for three days away, to give the population time to decide and to submit options for the preferential voting card.

3.8 THE LAST VOTE

The ship's passengers fill in their ballots, and although none of the worlds they've visited receive more than 50% of the primary vote, the recent world with genetically engineered pets is considered to be the least collectively offensive. Passengers must then decide whether they will stay with the ship as it makes its permanent home there, or whether they would like to disembark elsewhere and start from scratch – no guaranteed roof over their heads, few possessions, limited or no networks, no money. Kenji's family are content to stay with the ship, but the other scientists are more conflicted. Jackson feels tempted to return to his alien paramour, but would that be best for Nia? Grace and Cara each have other worlds they prefer, but can they bear leaving the ship for good?

3.9 DISEMBARKATION

La Vie En Mer is slowly losing passengers, dropping them off at familiar worlds with everything they can carry. With Nia's blessing, Jackson decides to pursue his romance with the purple-skinned alien, and after many hugs and well-wishes the two of them disembark into a cosmopolitan city of alien races. After his departure, Cara surprises both Grace and Kenji by revealing she'll be exiting at the all-women world, as it was simply where she felt most at home, and that she believes the previous networks she made will support her. She disembarks cradling Daniel's ashes in a pot.

3.10 LA VIE SUR TERRE

La Vie En Mer continues to lose its passengers to previous worlds. Grace and Ostari have decided to try their luck on the immortal world, although there's no guarantee that they'll be able to establish themselves there, and they're both visibly anxious about it. Anything they can't take with them has been gifted to Kenji's family, who are now very wealthy by *La Vie En Mer*'s standards. Grace pushes a cart of possessions off the ship as Ostari guides herself down in a wheelchair, into the unknown. Finally, Kenji is the only one of the four scientists still onboard the ship, along with more than half of its original population. They arrive at their ultimate destination and the ship celebrates with a boisterous party. His children have the biggest smiles on their faces. They are home.

REWIND

Juliette locks the caravan doors behind her, shutting out the mid-morning sun. She slips off her aviator sunglasses when she notices you're conscious, and her eyes look brighter than they ever did at school, like she's become fully alive out here. Maybe that's how all of the living will seem, now that you're a ghost.

"Hey, Lily." Juliette sounds gentle, but there's nothing tentative about it. "I found your body by the cliffs. I didn't touch it, but I thought your ghost might like somewhere friendly to wake up." She pauses, and then continues when you don't break the silence. "Or not. I mean, you're free to disappear at any time."

You glance again at the jars and wooden boxes lining the top shelves of the caravan walls. "You're a ghost killer," you say.

Some of the colour drains from her cheeks. "Well, my dad is. I help him sometimes. He gets contracts to hunt down the ghosts who can't function in society anymore, and they can't be controlled, so yes, we kill them." She offers a smile that you assume is supposed to be reassuring. "We don't kill ghosts who are just going about their business, not hurting anyone."

You lean forward on the caravan bed. "But you could."

Silence. Apparently this was not the response Juliette was expecting.

Do you trust Juliette?

> *Yes*

> *No*

> *REWIND*

You have selected Rewind.

The air in the train is too hot here, now that you've stepped outside of the cooled carriages intended for passengers. It hardly matters, though. This might be the last time you feel any temperature at all.

Your long cotton skirts brush against your legs as you approach the outside door. Through the pill-shaped window the lush mountains in the distance are almost still, but the dirt on the side of the tracks passes by at a break-neck blur. Soon there will be a stretch where there is almost no gap between the track and the sheer cliffs below, where the train borders a fall that no body could survive.

If this body dies now, days before schedule, then you will die on your own terms and in your own clothes, depriving your family of their ritual and the dress they decided your ghost will wear for all eternity. They will take some time to notice you're missing from the train, and then they will be busy with the festivities, meaning that it may be weeks before the ghosts find you.

You crumple the note in your left hand and grip the metal lever in your right. Opening the door takes less effort than you anticipated. The blustery wind rushes in, cooling your cheeks.

Do you step off the train?

> Yes

> No

> REWIND

You have selected Rewind.

There's a tiny blue spot on the white tablecloth from your blueberry parfait. You run a glossy fingernail over the blemish.

Juliette sits alone at a table on the other side of the dining car, reading and taking bites from a steak sandwich. Across your own table, Cara and Magdalene are comparing pictures of the necklaces their bodies will die in. It's currently fashionable to wear a red choker with dripping rubies, like your throat's been slit, even though their families would never allow that sort of death. They'll be drinking poison like good girls, so that no bloodstains can taint their ghostly forms.

You try to summon an enthusiastic smile to match theirs. It half works. Having them here should be a comfort, given you've seen Cara spill cake onto her bib at her first birthday party and you watched Magdalene toddle in the play pool with floaties on. But they've always wanted this: to give up their mortal forms at the appropriate age and marry the ghosts their families selected, securing their social statuses even more solidly, joining hundreds of their dead relatives in the eternal judgement of immortal high society.

You've been friends your whole lives. Now that each of your eldest siblings have all had healthy babies, there's no reason for your families to keep the three of you alive.

Juliette stands and offers you a small smile as she passes on her way out of the car.

Cara finishes sucking up the last of her iced coffee, which had been sloshing slightly with the movement of the train. "Oh, come to my room. I want to play you the new Gwen Libra song they're going to bury me to. If I move a chair, there's space enough to dance."

Magdalene rises from her seat.

"I'll catch up," you say.

Cara looks at you quizzically. "You sure, Lily?"

You nod, managing to smile. You pull a silver pin from your hair and tuck it into Cara's blonde locks, making her blush.

Once you're almost alone in the dining carriage, you allow your face to fall. Just a few days of freedom before you marry Wesley Conthrow, who died over twenty years ago and whose favourite conversation topic is 18th-century sports. Just a few days before you never have to sleep again, will never have any privacy, will never have any peace.

Forget death, all you want is some oblivion.

You wander over to the table Juliette was reading at earlier. A note is wedged under her dirty plate. Some scrawled travelling instructions on the back of the receipt for her steak sandwich: she's getting off at the next stop. Scholarship student. Not important enough to die this weekend.

Do you find Cara and Magdalene?

> Yes

> No

"We don't kill ghosts who are just going about their business, not hurting anyone."

You lean forward on the caravan bed. "But you could."

Do you trust Juliette?

> Yes

> No

> Rewind

OVERNIGHT, A FOREST GREW

Before the trees came, Andreas van Hoorft was one of the most famous perfumers in the world. He'd created the signature scents for world leaders, Olympians, TV personalities and billionaires. But more than that, he was known for his uncanny ability to recreate scents. He had only an average sense of smell but was exceptional at dividing that smell into parts. And with a small sample of someone's DNA he could grow their cells, their skin, their oils in his laboratory, which meant that with a little Andreas magic the average Melbourne Cup punter could smell exactly like their favourite movie star, footballer or supermodel.

His South Yarra laboratory had been three floors, with his personal quarters on the third and an impressive practical garden encompassing the rooftop. From inside the lush greenhouse I could see past the orchids and lilies to my own modest apartment nearby. Occasionally I wondered how big an influence that'd been on me getting the job; Andreas was big on convenience.

I was – and still am – Andreas's dutiful assistant. The main reason he had hired me was for my attitude, and nothing at all to do with my non-existent perfuming skills. He needed someone to keep the storerooms full, the plants fertilised, the coffee flowing, and occasionally to wine and dine a pop star until they'd let me swab their cheek for DNA, when he couldn't or didn't want to do so himself.

I enjoyed my job considerably, almost all of it, even with Andreas's eccentricities. He insisted on calling me Max, which was not my name, until everyone but my family and closest friends called me that, too. He took me shopping for men's suits and then had them tailored to fit me better. He preferred it when I kept my hair short. Clearly, he would have liked a male assistant, but had instead chosen the most appropriate person and was then adjusting them like one of my suit jackets.

Overnight, the forest grew.

I was one of the few that slept through it. Much earlier that evening I'd been having cocktails with beauty influencer Sarah-Blue Summer, at Andreas's request, and we'd gone back to my apartment because she wanted to play original Mario Kart. There had been more drinking. Shortly after she left in the early hours of the morning I'd passed out on the couch, which became a life-saving advantage when a huge wattle tree skewered my empty bed.

What was left of my apartment floor was covered with puffs of fluro yellow wattle flowers, architectural debris, pooled water, and showers of eucalyptus leaves. Two eucalyptus trees had shot up into my living room and into the apartment above, straight through the plaster and wood and concrete. The trees had carried my once ground-level apartment at least an additional floor into the air, and from that vantage point I could see through half-broken windows that there was barely a stretch of five metres anywhere without a tree in it. Outside did not smell like city anymore.

It smelt a lot more like the bush.

I had a terrible headache and was highly confused, but more than that I was angry. I was angry that my phone had no reception, that my sockets had no power, that the taps would not turn on for my morning shower. I forced myself to down some protein bars and Gatorade from the pantry, splashed myself with water from the toilet cistern, and changed into some clothes free from pollen dust.

After packing a bag I lowered myself from the window frame using a combination of car bungee cords and knotted bed sheets. I was on my way to the closest place that mattered: Andreas van Hoorft's laboratory.

There were some people on the street like me – some with bags, many in pyjamas, some bleeding. In the distance I could hear screams and a car alarm. One of South Yarra's designer boutiques had been spared by the trees and been looted instead. Closer to Andreas's there was a woman whose station wagon had been impaled by a eucalyptus and who was preparing to drop her baby into a pile of mattresses and onlookers' outstretched arms ten metres below.

When I arrived, Andreas was scavenging the wreckage of his building for anything that had survived the night. "Max!" he yelled when he saw me, and embraced me in his boxer shorts and a cashmere jumper, and kissed both my cheeks. His socks were soaked through with spilt perfume. All of his most valuable equipment lay in pieces: the machines he used to analyse and grow cells, the machine he used to alter DNA, the machine and associated computer program he'd recently commissioned to pull apart smells on his behalf, so that he could work twice as fast.

We salvaged what we could: perfume bases in plastic bottles; mint leaves that smelt like strawberries when you crushed them; most of the swabs; most of Andreas's handwritten notes; a surprisingly unblemished mandarin that also smelt like supermodel sweat.

Before long, my older sister Callie appeared where the front door used to be and said, "You have to come to Mum and Dad's. Dad didn't make it."

Through the chaos it was a ninety-minute walk to Mum and Dad's wooden bungalow. Andreas came with us, since all of his family was overseas and there wasn't anywhere more immediate he needed to be. Callie had biked to South Yarra and walked the mountain bike beside her while she shared the rest of the news.

Our gentle father, who had been involved in several forest conversation efforts, had nonetheless been lanced through the torso by a tree trunk. He had died very quickly. Our mother, who had been lying beside him at the time, was understandably inconsolable, and refused to leave the house or stray more than a few paces from Dad's body. This meant that Mum and our younger sister Hanna were still several metres in the air inside a broken box that looked like it might fall apart at any moment.

On arrival, Callie passed me her bike and scaled a branch-heavy tree that protruded into the kitchen. She had been a high school gymnast and always the most athletic of us. Andreas caught a piece of bark that Callie's foot dislodged, sniffed it, and declared it a lemon-scented gum.

While she was up there negotiating, Andreas and I catalogued the debris that had fallen from my childhood home: a photo of Mum, Dad and Hanna at Hamilton Island that had dropped off the fridge; one of Mum's wisteria earrings; a single five-kilogram dumbbell; a cracked Vanessa Amorosi CD; one of Dad's old polar fleece jumpers, worn down to half the original thickness. Andreas brought the jumper to his nose; I supposed that was how he got to know someone.

When Callie came down again it was with a sobbing, shaking Hanna following after her, but still no Mum.

Safely out of range of the house, the four of us passed around a box of Crimpy Chicken Shapes from our parents' pantry. Dad's death hadn't properly registered with me yet, but it obviously had for my sisters, who started telling stories about him: how his favourite food was Mum's homemade sausage rolls, how he'd needed surgery twice in the past three years from falling off his bike but still rode every week, how he liked to walk barefoot in spring and pluck nature strip daisies to make his family flower crowns. I mentioned how he wore Banana Boat sunscreen every day, religiously, and how he hummed the jingle when applying it. Andreas listened politely and asked questions like *where did he work* and *did he ever have a beard* and *what cologne did he wear*, which generated more stories.

We reminisced for hours. At one point Andreas excused himself, assuring me that he'd return, and was gone for the better part of the afternoon. When he re-emerged it was with a tiny plastic vial, which he pressed carefully into Callie's scraped hands.

"Please," he told her, "give this to your mother, and let her know that there's more of it down here."

Finally, Mum relented and came down safely.

It smelt exactly like Dad.

Andreas doesn't create celebrity perfumes anymore, and the concept of world-famous barely exists these days. Plenty of folks in south-east Melbourne know him, though, as the bloke who makes perfumes that smell like the old world.

Scent of McDonald's. Smell of summer barbeque and pool party. Eau de corporate office with expensive coffee machine. Movie theatre with choc-top ice creams and buttered popcorn. Sheets fresh from the dryer. Shopping centre food court.

Many people cry when they smell Andreas's perfumes now, which hardly ever happened before the trees came. And in addition to learning all the skills I need to survive in this new world, Andreas has actually started teaching me how to make perfume.

"Smell that, Max," he says, crushing some vanilla beans and lavender under my nose. "Now, what do we need next?"

WATCHHOUSE

Jenna Blythe is queer, so her family builds a Watchhouse: a long, thin building that runs parallel to the side of their primary mansion, with huge uncovered windows so there is limited privacy. From the mansion they can see almost everything, including into the Watchhouse bathroom, which is strategically placed to not be visible from the street, even if the Blythe's 6-foot stone fence fell down.

Then they bring in the 'pets': Alice and me, Class D members in the top 20% of wealth in the country. Wealthy enough that having us in the same rooms as Jenna wouldn't cause a scandal; poor enough that a Class A family snatching us off the street wouldn't cause one, either. I don't know Alice, but she looks vaguely familiar. We're both queer, too. Jenna is supposed to 'love and protect' us, otherwise we'll die. And honestly: we're definitely supposed to die while we're in the Watchhouse, sooner or later.

Jenna knows how this works. She's propped up the legs of the queen bed with four small wooden crates and shoved a mattress underneath for Alice and me to sleep on. The actual bed, where Jenna sleeps, is too exposed for us. If the Bythes across the manicured grass gain a clear view of a pet, then the hunt is on, and a fatal arrow flies out from the Watchhouse ceiling. They would rather shoot it themselves, of course, but there are two layers of window glass in the way, and they're too busy to stare at the Watchhouse all day. Instead, a surrogate AI Eye has been installed in each room, and if any of the Blythes are home, awake, and could theoretically have a line of sight to a pet, then it's programmed to shoot for them.

Jenna hands Alice and me plates of chocolate-spread sandwiches where we're hidden behind the back of the couch. The first time, she says, she disabled half the arrows and covered half the Eyes before the other Blythes barged in and cut the pets' throats.

This is the third time.

Jenna, Alice and I all have blackish hair and similar figures. This is more likely to be an intimidation tactic than a coincidence. The Eye isn't ever supposed to hurt Jenna, but we all look vaguely the same from behind.

Jenna is the only one of us allowed to leave. While she's out shopping or studying or seeing friends, Alice and I talk or read books or fill in logic puzzles with ballpoint pens. Jenna brings us Settlers of Catan to play together. Jenna brings us a Nintendo Switch. Behind the couch and under the bed are the safest places, but it's not really that hard to hide from the Eye. If you army crawl across the floor on the side of the room closest to the windows, it thinks the Blythes can't see you. The kitchen cupboards are purposefully too high for Alice and me to safely reach, but Jenna leaves food, plates and cutlery down on the floor.

Very occasionally, Jenna looks at me like she wants to kiss me, but it's only for a moment. This isn't the kind of situation that inspires romance.

I don't know why Alice stands up. We're both napping behind the couch, constrained by the protective nest of pillows and blankets we've built so that we don't move too far in our sleep – and then Alice isn't. I wake up in time to peek an eye out from the foot of the couch – in time to hear the swish of an arrow cutting through air and then the dull thunk as it nestles into her heart. Maybe she was sleepwalking. Maybe she just lost focus. I thought she was hanging on okay, mentally, but maybe she'd simply had enough, after all.

Jenna sleeps under the bed that night, on Alice's side of the mattress, with her back to me. She might be crying, but I can't see, and she speaks in approximately the same monotone as always.

"I'm a horrible person," she says.

I tell her none of this is her fault – she didn't build the Watchhouse, she didn't bring us here – but she says, "No, but I never make a final decision." Either she keeps her family, she says, and accepts their accompanying wealth and restrictions, or she cuts all those ties.

"You can build your own family," I say.

"And have no money and no influence, and have that family picked off the streets to die in Watchhouses?"

After that, we lie wordlessly in the under-bed gloom.

#

The Blythes across the grass have a Party with a capital P: loud and dripping with money and champagne. At just before sunrise in the quiet aftermath, I'm army-crawling back from pissing in the shower when I hear a rapid knock at the front door.

It's just me in the Watchhouse: Jenna will have been allowed to stay overnight in the primary mansion for once. I pick up the pace and beeline for the entrance, ignoring the resulting carpet burns.

"Riley," a familiar voice calls, hopefully not loud enough to disturb the Blythes. "Open the door. We'll get you out."

I pause behind the couch. The stretch of peach carpet between here and the door is completely exposed, and for the first time I'm truly terrified of the Eye mounted above the window. The Blythe mansion is silent; they're probably passed out drunk or safely asleep. But it's a lot to risk on 'probably'.

I bolt across the floor and stretch my arm up to the doorknob, certain an arrow is just about to impale the flesh above my elbow. I twist the glossy knob, drop my arm. No arrow comes. The door flies open instead and a bustle of allies, queer and straight alike, rush to circle me. All of their hair is a shock of rainbow colours, dyed or otherwise, so that the Eyes can't mistake them for me.

"Sorry we weren't here sooner," they say, and wrap me in a nondescript brown sack. "We had to figure out where you were, and then wait until it was safe."

They all carry me awkwardly outside in the middle of their circle, a brown lump in the middle of a colourful crowd, so that the Eyes outside don't transform me into a human pincushion. Pets are never allowed to leave – not ever – so the outside Eyes couldn't care less if the Blythes are awake or not.

But I do leave. I feel the gloriously smooth leather of a car seat underneath my skin, even with the sack in between, and we speed away.

I spot Jenna's Jeep on a mountain road a few months later. She takes slightly longer to recognise me, too. We keep glancing at each other, slowing down along the winding road until we've both stopped, her Jeep about thirty meters up the road from where we've parked my ageing sedan. My new girlfriend is in my passenger seat, and nods to herself as we climb out, saying, "Good not to get too close."

"Jenna," I call up the mountain, and it echoes slightly in the unpolluted air. "There's plenty of room in our back seat."

When we don't receive a reply, I add, "We're leaving in two minutes."

I glance down at my phone to check the time. Jenna keeps standing there, boots rooted to the leaf litter, the door of her Jeep wide open beside her.

LIGHT AND SLEEK AND STRONG

When I wake from having my breasts surgically removed, multiple apocalypses are in progress. The national news program playing opposite my hospital bed focuses on the hundreds of enormous fires ravaging the Australian landscape, but also touches on the deadly virus racing across Asia, the severe flooding throughout Europe, and the indiscriminate bloodlust that has struck America, driving frenzied citizens to brutally attack their family, friends and neighbours.

So this is it, I consider with toxic dissociation: the time I was out was the line between life and life's epilogue.

My sister had planned to be here when I woke, but obviously circumstances have changed. The hospital is barely running on a skeleton staff. Once I feel strong enough I pull away my oxygen mask and ease the intravenous drip from my wrist. I check the waterproof dressing they've attached to my chest, thankful that I don't seem to have needed a wound drain or a bladder tube. I toddle to the bathroom to piss and sip water from a cup beside the tap, then dress gingerly, still too drugged on painkillers to feel much more than exhausted and weak.

Even in the apocalypse, a tiny part of me is gratified to pull on my shoes and sock without my arms hitting my boobs.

And there they are, sitting on my bedside table in a large plastic jar sealed with biohazard tape: two huge discarded lumps of breast tissue. I paid extra to take them with me. If they were smaller they could've stayed on, but they had been approaching a H cup and I considered them a health hazard.

I pick up my breasts and walk myself home, while ash catches like snowflakes in my unwashed hair.

By the time I've struggled through my front door, social media is reporting a planet-destroying asteroid minutes away from colliding with

Earth. Seems like overkill, really. I collapse on the cold tiles of my bathroom where the halogen light above me is pleasantly, painfully bright. I study my biohazard breast tube where I've plonked it on the toilet seat. It doesn't seem very fair that the world is ending before I can properly remember moving without them shackled to my chest, but life has never been fair.

Something in the tube sparkles at me. The doctors washed down the tissue before they put it in the tube, and fat can be shiny, but it doesn't *glitter*.

I sit up awkwardly, rolling onto my side first to avoid using much of my upper body. There, lodged into the breast fat: the tiniest sliver of colour, canary yellow and sparkling. I retrieve my nail scissors and attack the seal on the jar until I can wrench it open. I am dimly aware of how deranged this would appear to an outsider, and perhaps I'm still delirious from the surgery, but apparently this is how I want to spend my last few minutes on earth.

I extract the canary yellow sparkle with tweezers. When it slides free it reveals itself to be a disc, perhaps three millimetres thick and roughly the size of my thumbnail. Translucent and glittery, like nail polish or rock candy; I have the sudden, overwhelming urge to put it in my mouth.

I check my phone. Asteroid hitting in five minutes now. The tiny disc slips past my lips, not tasting like much of anything, just the vaguest impression of cold animal fat. I swallow.

I dump the breast tissue out of the tube and onto the white tiles, ripping it apart with my scissors and tweezers. I find four other coloured discs of similar size – candy-coloured orange, purple, green, and pink – and swallow them all. Then I lie myself back down, close my eyes and wait to die.

Death seems to take an awfully long time, and there's only so long you can be shit-scared without the danger coming to pass.

I may have fallen asleep. When I eventually check my phone the asteroid has magically changed course, the fires have extinguished, the floods have dried up, and the virus and bloodlust victims – those who haven't already died – have recovered. Nobody understands what is happening and everyone is crying with grief and/or relief, or they're like me and throwing up bile into the toilet bowl.

#

Two days later, I am more settled on the toilet when my phone informs me that the asteroid is back, the fires are back, and I may as well lie down again and wait to die.

On auto-pilot, I stand and look at my shit in the toilet bowl like I have every other day of my life. As my hand reaches toward the flush, I see a purple glint amongst the mess in the bowl and immediately freeze. Two instances don't quite make a pattern, but...

I hurry to pull on some latex gloves and lay a large garbage bag on the bathroom floor. On top of the garbage bag I sift through the shit for the candy-coloured discs, and before long I am amazed to find all five.

I rinse off the discs and douse them in Listerine, which will have to suffice given the apocalypse is imminent. I scoot out onto the balcony to see the asteroid hanging in the sky like a guillotine razor, and then place the discs onto my tongue and close my lips.

The asteroid veers dramatically to my left.

Well, then.

I spend the next three days shitting directly onto a garbage bag, which is far from the glamorous kind of ways one imagines saving the world. While I am waiting for the discs to re-emerge I am convincing my cousin the vet that I need him to secure the discs inside me in some way. This is much easier to do once the discs leave me again and I can visually demonstrate.

My cousin sews the discs under the skin of my right thigh. The skin above the discs never bounces back quite the same way as it used to, but the same apocalypses never come back, either.

My thigh heals faster than my chest, so they end up recovering around the same time. The world is still trying to rebuild itself. If I knew that removing my breasts was going to lead to such catastrophe I never would have gone ahead with it, but now there's no use crying over spilt breast tissue.

When I leave my front door I feel light and sleek and strong. I can breathe and move so much more easily. And under the clear sky, for the first time since I started adolescence, I start to run.

FAEWILD

The following is an account of highly illegal activities related to breaches of Faewild, the realm, by Miss Emory Knight and related parties.

At the start of the beginning, Emory was sprinting towards an abandoned plot of land not far from her home. It looked like it had been an assisted living facility or halfway house before being condemned. By the time Emory was twelve, the ochre and cream paint colours had faded and chipped, and all the boxy buildings were partially hidden by overgrown branches and vines.

Panting from deep in her lungs, Emory slipped through the wire fencing that blocked off the abandoned land and raced through the thicket of grasses towards the steps of the main building. The contents of her backpack jumbled and rattled as she ran. Wilson and his friends weren't far behind: she could hear them part the fence with a metallic scrape just as she threw herself inside the main door.

[With hindsight, this had been a terribly foolish thing to do. Emory would have been much safer finding a nearby adult and seeking protection with them. Similarly, Wilson and the boys were not going to *kill* her. They might have thrown a punch where her uniform would've hidden the bruise, but all they really wanted was the contents of her bag. Surrendering would have been much more sensible, but Charlie *needed* the parcel she'd picked up from the Post Office; her parents didn't have the money for a replacement.]

She holed herself up in what looked like it could've been a storage closet, three flights of stairs up inside the main building. It was almost entirely dark, and Emory was trying to be as quiet as possible. Parts of the grasses outside had stuck to her socks. The boys were crashing about downstairs looking for her, yelling her name. The building wasn't big enough to hide her for much longer.

Desperate as a wolf in a trap, Emory reached for the only possibility she could think of: she ripped open Charlie's parcel and pulled out the jar of Portal Salve. She dipped her fingers in: the salve was black and viscous, like honey without the sugar. She smeared it across the ceiling at the back of the closet, where the roof sloped down to about head height.

With her clean hand, she reached inside the parcel again and grasped a Fae Cube, a transparent, hard plastic box a little larger than her fist. It was a little stout to properly be a cube. She gripped the box with sweaty fingers, held her breath, and then pushed through the patch of Portal Salve on the ceiling, all the way up to her wrist.

It worked. She deposited the Fae Cube on the lip of the other side of the portal and carefully retracted her hand. Then she waited as long as she dared.

[It is important to note here that opening a portal to the Faewild in an uncontrolled environment is considered reckless endangerment of the entire community, akin to committing arson in the middle of bushfire season, and Emory was exceedingly lucky that nothing life-threatening emerged from that portal during the minute or so it was open.]

The boys downstairs had gotten louder, like they may have ascended to the next floor. The salve on Emory's dirty hand had already begun to dry and crack, and deciding that she couldn't wait any longer, she crossed her fingers amongst the flakes so tightly that her joints hurt. Then she retrieved the Fae Cube from within the portal and felt in the darkness for the latch. Miraculously, it had flipped to horizontal, for locked. Something was inside. Relief flooded her whole body like plunging into a hot spring; she had *caught* something.

She tore the portal from the ceiling like melted wax ripped off her mother's legs, partially so nothing else could come in, and partially so that her prize couldn't escape back out. The portal's crumpled remains were discarded to a corner of the tiny room, inert. Then she twisted the latch of the Fae Cube so its lid sprung open and its contents burst out.

The first thing she saw was the three eyes, glowing dimly milky white amongst its black backdrop. They were at roughly chin height, close enough for her to reach out and touch if she had wanted to. Then she could make out the rest of the creature, lit by the subtle radiance of its eyes: a delicate, vulpine face with six thick prehensile whiskers; two small antlers; a long body covered in grey, shimmering scales like sequins; two squat little claws at the front like a t-rex and no back legs; a shoestring tail. It was hovering in the air with seemingly no effort, and gauzy clouds had started to form around its body.

Emory had never seen this variety of faewild in real life, but it was #314 in the faewild encyclopedia she'd had memorised for three years. *Fog dragon.*

The boys sounded mere meters away now. There was a protracted screech from beyond the door that could've been someone dragging a branch against a window.

"Hello," whispered Emory to her fog dragon. "I love you. Please scare them away."

She swung open the door, tongue bitten between her teeth, and the fog dragon twisted in the air towards daylight. As it flew into the hall it grew rapidly in size, so by the time it disappeared from Emory's sight its body was so wide she wouldn't have been able to wrap her arms all the way around it.

There was another final crash from the boys, some alarmed cursing, and then the screams began. They were soon replaced by heavy footfalls and a slammed front door, which then sounded like it broke from its rusted hinges and thudded to the floor like a fallen tree.

Emory crept from her hiding place. The fog dragon twisted back towards her and was shrinking again. "Thank you," said Emory. "Thank you for saving my life." It watched her with unblinking, milky eyes and continued to shrink until it could've fitted in her cupped hands, and then nestled itself in her shirt pocket, right next to her heart.

At the start of the middle, Emory was eighteen and had wrangled herself a scholarship for Sprywood College for Faewild Studies. Initially, they had hand-delivered her rejection in a gold envelope on her eighteenth birthday, making it the worst birthday of her life. Her entrance exam had been excellent, her academic marks above average, but her overall experience with faewilds officially low. Her parents had no faewilds of their own, had spent their limited extra money on Charlie's faewild ambitions, and then, even after Charlie's disappearance when Emory was fifteen, had taken too long to find the money for her to legally catch a faewild of her own at a Gateway Centre.

Unofficially, she'd been playing with, riding, and training a fog dragon for six years in secret. The fog dragon was worth substantially more than her parents' house, and if anyone saw it they would understandably ask where she'd gotten it, in the same tone that they'd ask why a working-class child had the keys to a top-of-the-range Porsche. Then it would have been taken away (best case) or she would've been imprisoned for how she'd acquired it (worst case), so in the end she'd mailed its Fae Cube to herself for her eighteenth birthday, to be a (not so) surprising present from a (not so) mysterious benefactor.

Then she'd ridden her fog dragon to the office window of Sprywood College's Head of Admission, feeling like real a wanker in the process, and convinced him to overturn her original rejection and add her to the very top of the waiting list. Emory's supposed ability to bond with and train a fog dragon in just a few days made her look like a prodigy. In the end, thanks to one of its existing students falling ill and dropping out, she'd only started the academic year a week later than her classmates.

It was enough to single her out. On Emory's second day at Sprywood, a freckled blonde girl slid a takeaway hot chocolate across Emory's desk before their Health & Care class, and in a soft, clear voice, asked, "So I hear you have a fog dragon?"

The girl's name was Lea. She wore polished oxfords and the kind of lush, expensive sweater that made Emory extra self-conscious about her own thrift store vest. But Lea didn't seem to care. Emory liked her immediately, the way that Emory usually liked faewilds immediately. Occasionally, during the lesson, one of them would smile at the other behind their takeaway cups. Afterwards, they compared handwritten notes, and Emory shared theories on how faewild physiology reflected the Faewild realm, and Lea brought up how human culture and health was being affected by faewilds in a kind of symbiosis.

Soon, they were talking together every day. They dissected ideas for hours, and played elaborate card games, and Emory took Lea up on the fog dragon, sitting Lea in the front so she could hold onto the antlers for security. Nestled into Lea from behind, Lea smelt like mint and raspberries and sugar. From in the sky above the college, everything was beautiful.

Then they were walking with linked pinky fingers as they crossed the campus, or sitting with them entwined in their shared classrooms. Lea was conveniently left-handed, so both of them still had their free hands to write with. For a while, everything was perfect – and then there was that asshole, Sebastian Slater.

For several weeks, despite his significant popularity, both Emory and Lea were largely unaware of Sebastian's existence. Neither had noticed a pattern of Lea providing better or more detailed answers than him in class, because neither of them had noticed him at all. Sebastian, however, had certainly noticed being embarrassed and overshadowed, and his mild irritation had grown throughout the semester into a simmering rage, ultimately leading to him cornering Lea on her way back from Techniques & Training.

"Faewild fight," he spat, "9:00 PM tomorrow, Court C."

Emory had wanted to alert their professors. Battling faewilds required a special license, one that none of them were eligible for until after they'd passed certain end-of-semester exams. It wasn't as catastrophic as opening up an unauthorised portal to Faewild, the realm, but it was still illegal, and Emory was already full of those kinds of secrets.

The two of them sat on Lea's bed. Lea was solemn but confident, her hands deep in the fur of her two primary faewilds, a fireshot and a phase fox. "I have to fight him, Em. If I don't do it this way, he'll find a way to hurt me or mine more directly. Hopefully, when I win, he'll leave me alone."

Emory fingered her worn leather bracelet that used to be Charlie's. Had her brother dealt with similar challenges before he vanished from Sprywood? What would he have done in their place?

The Sports Centre, and Court C, was unlocked for them: Sebastian worked there sometimes, cleaning equipment and running the occasional spin class, and had the right keys. His faewild, a chromatica, was circling Court C's court, and had literally shat inside the netball goal circle. The chromatica resembled a crow the size of a Saint Bernard, with two sets of eagle-like talons that could've cut Emory's neck in an instant. At first glance, it looked to be blind, but then you noticed that its tail fanned out like a peacock's, and that tail was covered in dozens of eyes.

Lea had brought her fireshot to the battle, slung loosely around her neck like an animated scarf. Fireshots resembled a mix of ferret, otter and opossum, a little less long than one of Lea's legs, and about as wide as her calf. Four large, solid fangs protruded like an overbite from its upper jaw. It had been kneading holes into Lea's sweater in anticipation, and a couple of blue threads had worked their way around its claws. Lea ducked her head to whisper final instructions.

Sebastian wasted little time. It began.

They were decent battlers, both of them, for teenagers who were not supposed to have battled faewilds before. But Lea was better. Sebastian had made a strategic error choosing the Sports Centre, where his chromatica could not fly for long enough to build up much speed, and where the fireshot could use the walls as leverage to launch itself at the chromatica. If they had been outside, he might have won.

As it was, the battle was a long series of attempted attacks and evasive manoeuvres, punctuated by the occasional significant hit. The fireshot ignited its back and belly mid-air and fell through the chromatica's feathered tail, burning through a third of its eyes, which fell to the shining floor in ash. The chromatica nicked the fireshot just above its hind leg, leading to an arc of blood next to the edge of the basketball court. Finally, the fireshot caught the chromatica from a blind spot and closed its fiery fangs around one of its legs, almost severing the talon clean off.

When Sebastian didn't show immediate signs of conceding, Emory stepped forward and yelled, "Enough! Put it in the cube! Do you want it to lose the claw?"

He shot her a look of utter disgust, but it seemed to break the spell. A couple of seconds later, the chromatica had retreated to the stasis of its Fae Cube. She hoped he'd bring it out later, once he had his battling license, and get it surgically seen to.

They left the Sports Centre for Sebastian to clean. Back in Lea's room, after rinsing the fireshot's wound and assessing it as relatively shallow, they applied a padded dressing and wrapped it with a bandage from Lea's first aid kit. The fireshot seemed unfazed, and made a rumbling sound Lea said was its equivalent to purring. She had caught it at a Gateway Centre when she was ten, and Emory was jealous.

They put it back in its Fae Cube overnight, just in case its health took a turn for the worst while Lea was asleep. And then Emory went back to her own room, which she regretted ever after.

Emory was woken by the chilly paws of Lea's phase fox in its incorporeal form. They had switched rooms mid-semester so that Lea's room was directly above Emory's, and often used the phase fox to pass semi-translucent messages through the floor. This time, there was no incorporeal slip of paper – just the urgent batting of Emory's face, and then the phase fox floated over to the bedroom door, waiting for her.

Emory leapt out of bed in her worn tartan pyjamas, grabbed her mobile phone, and then hurried after the phase fox. Upstairs, Lea's door was closed. Emory yanked it open, flicked the lights: the bed was empty, the crimson bed-covers half pulled onto the floor. The phase fox flew under the bed and merged back with its solid body, which immediately started nipping at the floorboards. Emory saw them then: a small group of acid ants, each the size of one of her hands, were wandering around the room dripping acid behind them. Parts of the floor and curtains were smoking. The acid would start eating through into Emory's room before long.

She had never seen a truly wild faewild before; the domesti-spray that calmed them when they were first captured in Fae Cubes at least gave you a neutral position to start a relationship from, although of course they could grow aggressive and abdicate if you broke their trust.

A shiny spot of black poked out from behind the dishevelled bed covers. Emory's heart dropped. With closer inspection, a rough circle of Portal Salve had been smeared on the ground beside Lea's bed, where someone might have put a water glass if they wanted to dip the sleeper's fingers in it.

Emory's thoughts swirled like a cyclone. She forced herself to breathe deeply, and then took out her phone to text her parents, plus a few friends on campus: *Faewild breach in Lea's room. Send help.*

The help would only be coming for *their* realm. No-one had ever travelled to the Faewild realm for more than a couple of minutes and returned.

Emory patted the chest pocket of her pyjamas, where the fog dragon was still curled against her chest. She grabbed the fireshot's Fae Cube out of Lea's bedside drawers for good measure, and left the phase fox to dismantle the acid ants before they caused too much damage to the building.

Then she knelt on the floor and pushed herself face-first into the dark portal. Down into Faewild.

At the start of the end, Emory climbed to her feet inside Faewild, the realm, and it was grey. After the crimson, navy and gold of Lea's bedroom, Faewild looked like someone had shifted the world's saturation dial close to monochrome. Even Faewild sun, hanging low in the sky, was a pale blonde rather than the marker-yellow or deep gold Emory remembered.

She had emerged in a patch of scrub and grasses, which was itself in the middle of an eclectic forest. A variety of pale trees were sprinkled haphazardly across the landscape, the equivalents of species that Emory didn't think would naturally grow together: pines and eucalyptus and oaks and huge succulents.

There was movement on the floor: more acid ants, dozens of them, and Emory quickly tapped her pocket to dislodge her fog dragon. The dragon grew quickly, but even as she jumped to mount it a small stream of ant acid splashed her bare toes. While the pain took a moment to register, her body immediately wanted to contort, and it took all of her willpower to get herself balanced properly on the back of the fog dragon. As they rose she allowed herself to hiss, to bury her head against the dragon's scaly neck. Her left foot hung limp to one side. It still felt like it was actively burning, and the two smallest toes were simply gone.

They were barely four metres in the air when other ghostly shapes floated up from the grasses: the incorporeal forms of three wild phase foxes. They'd obviously been stalking Emory for the handfuls of seconds she'd been on the ground, and now that she was airborne they had followed in the appropriate form, clearly hoping to knock her from the sky to a position that their flesh-and-blood bodies could feast on.

"Fog," Emory snapped. "Fly."

The fog dragon shot away from the phase foxes. Emory clutched its antlers with pale knuckles, her head still tucked into its neck and her knees digging into its sides. As they flew, the frigid rush of air shocked her maimed foot and then swiftly numbed it. Soon the misty sky around them thickened to a deep fog, and the fog dragon twisted in the air and chose another direction to lose their pursuers. They switched directions twice more before the dragon slowed and Emory felt her immediate panic subside. Then it was time to find Lea.

They found her before it was completely dark. Lea's body was draped over a small hill, stomach-up and un-moving, and from the air Emory was struck with the horrific realisation that she was likely looking at a corpse. Intellectually, she had known that was the most probable outcome, but actually seeing it was a different matter.

She guided the fog dragon down at speed and the details emerged: Lea's blonde hair fanned around her head like a messy halo, already interspersed with flowering weeds like someone had deliberately woven them through. Her eyes were closed, face sallow, yellow pollen on her lips. On her left side more weeds had wrapped themselves around her fingers like rings, around her wrists like bracelets. On her right side that hand seemed to have sunk into the earth completely, and her arm was only visible from the mid-forearm up.

As she slid off, Emory realised that the same thing was true of Lea's left leg. It wasn't just bent underneath her: everything below the knee had been swallowed into the ground itself.

Emory awkwardly hobbled towards Lea, favouring her injured foot. The grief and terror overshadowed the physical pain, but walking was still tricky. She knelt and felt for a pulse, forcing herself to concentrate. Lea's neck was living-warm. The pulse was still there, if faint. Emory let out a shaky groan, and then cupped Lea's cheek, calling her name. There was no response.

Emory turned her attention to the rest of Lea. She wiped the pollen from Lea's lips with her pyjama sleeve and released Lea's hair from its entanglement. Lea's right hand was truly submerged deep in the soil. A gentle tug would not free it. In the end, Emory placed both feet on either side of Lea's right arm and pulled with all her might, and the hand finally popped out like a flower pulled out by the roots.

The hand, now freed, was dangerously red and raw, and tiny pinpricks of blood were starting to bloom across its surface where they mixed with the last bits of powdery soil. There was a clear red line across Lea's forearm demarcating which flesh had been buried. If they had been at home, Emory would have known what to do. For now, she lay Lea's injured arm across her stomach as carefully as she could, and hoped she wasn't making things any worse.

The fog dragon had shrunk a little when they'd landed, but it had grown again and was now circling Emory and Lea, snapping its jaws defensively at unseen aggressors beyond the trees, and shrouding everything in a ten-metre radius in a low mist. Emory studied it for a moment, trying to get her breath back, and then concentrated on Lea's still-buried leg. They needed to get out of here.

But no matter how hard Emory pulled, adrenaline-filled and sweating and grunting, Lea's leg would not budge. It was like it had grown into the ground. Emory knelt in the grass and clawed at the soil around it with her fingers, which initially proved more effective, but the new parts of Lea's leg that she unearthed were a horror: bright red and shining like uncooked meat, with strong roots the size of her pinky finger impaled deep in Lea's flesh. Emory had to suppress the reflex to vomit.

She slumped in the dirt, stained and crying, while the fog dragon continued to snap its jaws nearby. Then she pulled the fireshot's Fae Cube from the deep pocket of her pyjama pants, twisted the latch, and watched the fireshot bound over to Lea's side.

"I can't free her, fireshot." Emory's voice was monotone. "But you might be able to."

The fireshot sniffed avidly around Lea, her leg, and the surrounding hill, alternately whimpering and growling, and finally stared up at Emory.

"I don't like it one bit, either, but I don't see another way we're all getting out of here."

There was a tense moment of silence broken by unnatural screeching in the trees. Emory's sweat was suddenly chilly on her skin.

The fireshot started frantically digging around Lea's leg, paws blurring, and Emory thought it may have misunderstood. But it was simply making itself some more room. Once about six inches of Lea's leg had been re-exposed it ignited its fangs, casting the hill in fiery glow, and snapped its jaws. Everything below Lea's knee was severed instantly.

Emory hurried to check the wound, which had cauterised nicely, and thank the fireshot, whom she tucked back in its Fae Cube for safekeeping.

Lea's eyelids fluttered. Emory was thrilled to hear her name again, even if it came out raspy and weak from Lea's throat. Emory cleared the last vines from Lea's body, scooped her up as best she could, and called for the fog dragon.

They didn't go back the way they'd come. Even if they could've found where they'd entered, the chance that a portal was still open in the same place was microscopic. Instead, they simply flew through the deep dusk – it never seemed to get fully dark in Faewild – to a river where Emory hurried to clean their wounds without incident.

Once her injury had properly registered, Lea had begun to cry: the sort of strange, tearless weeping Emory might've expected from someone medically sedated. Lea said almost nothing, and in response Emory found the words pouring out of her – too many words – trying to explain and justify and apologise, and ultimately shut her mouth because she was probably just making things worse.

She felt the darkness and loss leaking out of Lea like a physical presence, and felt her own deep heartache, and then intentionally set all of that aside until she could better concentrate on their immediate safety.

Soon after ascending again, she spotted a thin plume of smoke.

A single stream of smoke, as if released by a chimney, seemed curious enough in Faewild that it warranted investigation. Lea was still very weak, so she was propped between Emory's legs at the front of the fog dragon, and they flew with one of Emory's hands on the antlers and one around Lea's waist.

As one would expect, the smoke came from a fire, and the fire came from a cave atop a small sandstone cliff. A makeshift rope ladder had been secured around a tree and was hanging off the edge of the cliff nearby. Inside the cave appeared to be a human man.

The man had been eating some freshly cooked spinehare meat prior to their arrival, but had frozen in place upon seeing two teenage girls riding a fog dragon, which was now hovering near the mouth of the cave.

They all stared at one another. Illuminated by the dying flames, the man's hair was longer than fashionable, shorn unevenly around his neck. Both his nose and arm looked like they'd been broken some time ago and hadn't healed quite right. His uncovered skin was covered in scars of varying shapes and sizes, as though a small child had tried to draw them on as tiger stripes, and he was missing at least three of his fingers.

When he stood and approached the fog dragon, he did so with a slight but noticeable limp. "Emory?" he asked, in a strange voice that was out of practice.

She almost lost her grip on the antler. "Charlie?"

They saved most of the conversation for the morning. Once Lea had determined it was safe to do so, she'd sunk into an exhausted slumber, and was still sleeping while Emory and Charlie spoke quietly around the ashes of the fire. Charlie's primary faewild, a zeabeer with one remaining eye, kept watch near the mouth of the cave.

It hadn't been Charlie's idea to enter Faewild. He and another classmate, Melissa Harden, had been approached by two of the richest students in his year level and offered $10,000 each if they could cross over to Faewild, the realm, for just sixty seconds. Charlie had been skipping breakfast and eating twenty-cent packets of ramen noodles for dinner every day. He'd needed the money, and he'd wanted to send some back home for Emory and their parents, too. And it was only supposed to be sixty seconds.

Melissa had gone through the portal first, and then Charlie had followed her. The first thirty seconds had been tense, with glowing eyes blinking through the dark undergrowth around them, but he didn't think either of them had been hurt. Then he'd turned around and Melissa was gone – and so had the portal. He still didn't know whether something had gone terribly wrong, or whether they'd all left him there intentionally.

Emory shook her head. She'd never heard of any Melissa, and neither of those rich kids had ever said anything. "Now you can finally come home, after all, and find out."

He stared at her sadly. "I've been here for years, Emory. I don't think we're leaving."

"Maybe," she said, trying to sound more confident than she felt. "You didn't have a fog dragon before, and you didn't have me, who's memorised the percentage of faewild species that come through our nearest Gateway Centre. And now Lea and I have you, who I'd bet knows this place better than any other human alive."

She clearly had his attention. Emory took a deep breath and continued, "30% lopefoot, 25% acid ants, 20% spinehare, 15% drape heron, 10% zeabeer. Do you know that place?"

His face showed it clicking together. "That's half a day's walk away."

She beamed. "Quicker on the dragon."

#

The three of them climbed onto the fog dragon, Charlie behind Emory behind Lea. Wherever there was a Gateway Centre, people would be regularly opening portals in heavily controlled environments. Usually, whatever was captured in those Fae Cubes was from a subset of faewilds that naturally lived in that area, but once in a blue moon there was a notable exception.

The three of them were hoping to be that exception now.

The fog dragon wove back and forth over their target area; the equivalent of palm trees and cacti and weeping willows co-existing in Faewild's perpetual grey. Emory kissed the back of Lea's pale neck, hoping she'd hold on a little longer. They all scoured the ground for portal-sized black patches. It took some time, and some luck.

But since you're reading this, well – you know we found one.

Please be kind in your judgement.

The above statement has been declared a true and accurate account by Emory Knight (currently on remand) on the 4th day of April 2024.

THE WHITE FACTORY

One day in late spring, 108 women named Nicole gather outside a large white building that was once a factory. Within the first five minutes we discover we share the same name, and after that it takes only slightly longer to uncover that we had all had our 27th birthday exactly two weeks ago.

A lady in a glossy red coat checks our gilded invitations and photo IDs, and then ushers us one by one inside the converted factory. Once my eyes adjust to the dimness inside I see a smiling androgynous person holding a thin silver chain towards me.

With all 108 of us inside, the woman in the red coat follows and closes the door after her. Without the bright sunlight I can see that this central space breaks off into three corridors to our north, east and west. The space is completely white: no signage, no adornments.

Red Coat welcomes us and explains the rules: our silver necklaces are for collecting engraved, coloured metal rings. Different rings can be found throughout the building. We have ninety minutes to collect as many as possible before convening back here at 3:00 PM. The five Nicoles with the most rings after ninety minutes will each receive $3000 and the opportunity for another prize which is not yet revealed.

She answers several questions. Stealing rings from others will result in immediate disqualification. Actively hindering others will result in immediate disqualification. Being late to the finish at 3:00 PM will result in immediate disqualification. Lastly, only one of each ring will be counted at the end, so there's no need to keep multiples of the same colour and engraving.

Red Coat fires her starting pistol straight into the air, and the 108 of us rush into the corridors like liquid into empty pipes.

#

Room One.

I race straight towards the elevator at the end of the western hall and ride it to the third floor. Only a handful of others accompany me.

Once I run far enough to leave them behind I choose the first door available. A bouquet of pink oriental lilies blooms on a table in the centre of the room, and all along the walls vines weave across trellises, with closed lilies drooping from the vines three or four metres up.

I dig my fingers and toes into the trellis and clamber towards the ceiling, searching inside the closed petals for a ring, and finding it tucked inside the third bud I try. I snap the yellow ring securely to my silver necklace.

Engraved inside the ring is the word POSSIBILITY.

Room Two.

The sliding door to this room shuts firmly behind me; there is a big green button to manually exit. On the walls are three plaques with riddles engraved:

My eyebrows evolved to speak with you, you'll hear me tapping on your floor, I am the opposite of god, I'll scratch to get inside your door.

"A dog," I say, and hear a bell.

I am a bow you cannot wear, and you may see me when it's wet, you cannot touch me so don't try, I'll always be a little bent.

"A rainbow," I say. Another bell.

A witch told me your name but we are strangers.

"Nicole," I half-guess, but surely it has to be. There is a congratulatory chime, and a pale blue ring pops out of an indentation in the wall.

Room Three.

There is a pedestal with a large keyhole in this room. Nothing else. I move on.

Room Five.

I dive into a pool to retrieve an orange ring, splashing my discarded cotton sundress in the process. I exit with soaking underclothes and my hair in a knot, and my feet dripping puddles onto the white concrete.

Room Seven.

I can't find anything obviously hidden in the lone piano, and I can't even begin to read the sheet music clipped open at its front.

I make a deal with the Nicole I see hovering by the door: the ring in the piano for a copy of the orange ring at the bottom of the swimming pool. As she rolls her wheelchair over to the ivory keys, I study the silhouetted fir trees tattooed in a line across her shoulders.

Room Three II.
Once I am close enough, I see the hint of something glinting at the end of the eastern corridor. A skinny door frame has been installed in front of the white bricks, and when I feel along the top of the frame my fingers hit the solid cold of a hefty key.

I take the key to the room with the keyhole pedestal. The key clicks into place perfectly. Star clusters are projected onto the ceiling, and the pedestal allows me to unpack it piece by piece like a puzzle box until a ruby ring emerges.

Room Ten.
Three forty-something women perch in a circle around a heating cauldron. They usher me in and ladle me a cup of mulled wine, then interview me for a few minutes about my job, my interests, and my political views. They're beaming at me. The brunette wipes the last of the pool from my face with a handkerchief, while the redhead fetches my ring from the cauldron with a magnet and fishing wire.

Room Thirteen.
A completely dark room. I stumble about as carefully as I can for a few minutes, running into pillows and furniture and what seem to be children's toys. I run my hands over and into everything, hoping to expose their secrets while still building a mental map of the room.

Eventually I grasp the foamy texture of a cupcake bottom and accidentally coat my fingers in thick, sticky icing. I bite through the cupcake's body and spear the ring inside on my tongue.

At the end of the northern corridor is a young girl with a scraped knee who asks me for a band-aid. I fish inside my satchel for my beaten-up packet. She trades me a candy-pink ring.

I won't guide you through every one of my rooms. There is a perfume-making room where I fail, and trivia and finish-a-poem rooms where I succeed. There is a room where I have tea with a teenager who asks me about my past relationships and then latches a ring to my necklace himself.

The important thing, in the end, is that I make it back to the meeting area with three minutes to spare, and with twenty-one rings, which looks like quite a respectable number indeed.

After checking for duplicates and legitimacy, Red Coat takes the five Nicoles with the highest ring counts, including myself, into an adjacent room I didn't notice before. The afternoon sun illuminates an antique chair on a raised platform, which would not be out of place as a throne in a professional theatre production. A tall, striking woman in a grey pinstripe suit and crimson lipstick rises from the chair, and all eyes are immediately drawn to her.

"Welcome and congratulations," she says, and her voice is smooth and deep. "I know the competition today was not an easy one, and I'm very grateful to you all for participating. Phoenix..." She turns her gaze to the androgynous person we met at the building entrance. "Please give our winners their cash prizes as a token of our appreciation."

Phoenix gifts us each a gold envelope with a wad of hundred dollar bills tied together with ribbon. It is solid in my hands, easily the most amount of cash I have seen in my life.

The woman waits for us to stop admiring our prizes before she continues: "Which brings me to my key order of business for the day." She tucks a hand into the pocket of her slacks. "As you may have gathered from today's theatrics, I am not someone for whom money is much of a hindrance. But I do struggle to find the right people to include in my circle, so I paid a psychic to tell me the details of my future wife." She pauses for a second while my heart rate spikes dramatically.

"So my name is Clementine," she says, "and one of you in here or out there is almost certainly going to be the woman I marry."

My hand has sweated a translucent window through the gold envelope. Now that she has introduced herself, I recognise Clementine as the founder of the Australian Society for Endangered Animals.

Red Coat lines us up in order of rings collected. There are three Nicoles with more rings than I managed, and they all get the chance to speak before me.

But the first Nicole is straight.

The second Nicole declines, saying Clementine isn't her type.

The third Nicole is the one with the fir tree tattoo, and is already married.

And then I'm staring at Clementine as she's approaching me, with her heart-shaped face and strong cheekbones and radiant smile. My sundress is askew and my hair is a mess and the swimming pool water has washed off most of my makeup, but she doesn't look like she minds. I fight the ridiculous urge to curtsy in front of her.

"I would very much like to get to know you better," I manage to say, "with the intention of looking forward towards marriage, maybe, if things go well." I glance up – she's grinning at me with perfect teeth – and glance down again. "If that would please you, too."

"I'd be delighted," she says.

Clementine has a very comfortable car take me home. I stretch out in the back seat and read the engravings inside the rings on my necklace – POSSIBILITY, COMPASSION, RESILIENCE – and slip them over my fingers, one by one.

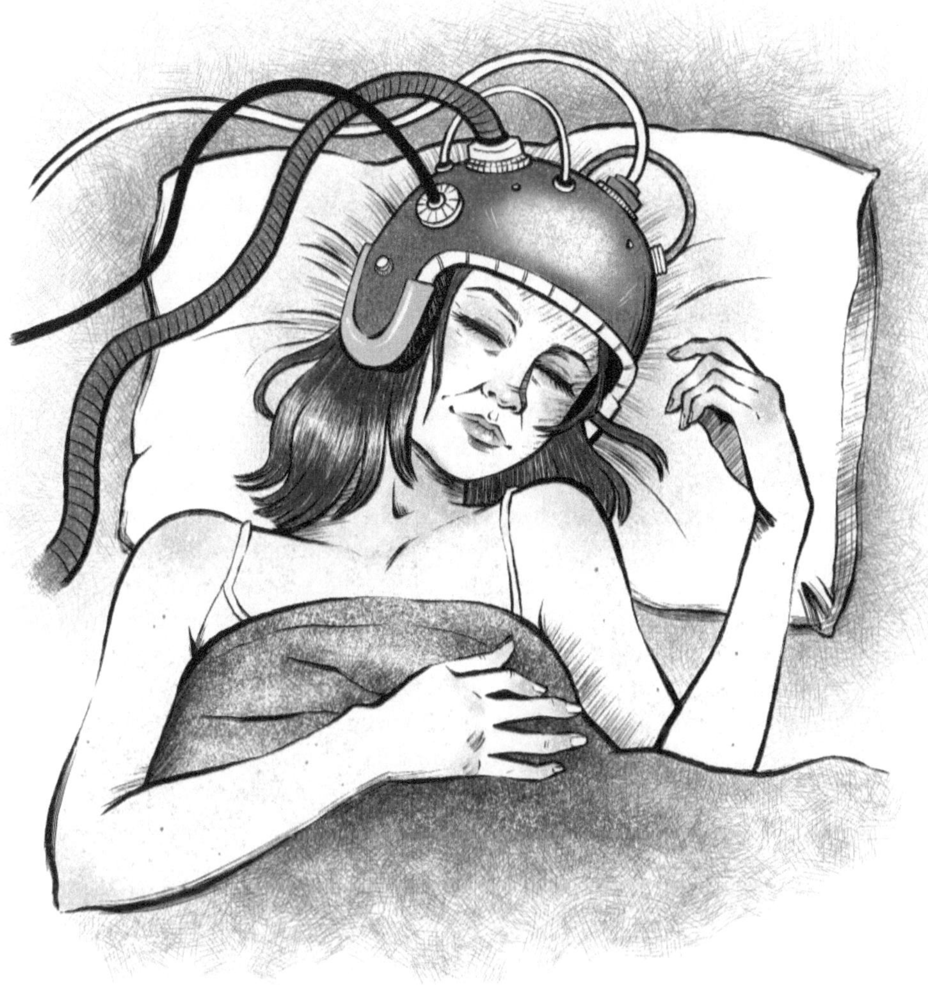

NEURO

Neuros have become increasingly mainstream over the past couple of years. Four months ago, when I decided to write this article, 34% of 18 to 55-year-olds owned their own Neuro. I'd never considered myself a Luddite in the past, but there comes a point where you have to admit you're behind the times when it comes to modern technology. So if you know next to nothing about Neuros (like I did), don't worry and read on – I spent the last four months researching them so you don't have to.

BUYING A NEURO

Very early on, I visited my local big-box technology store to scope out the purchasing situation. A bald and bearded man called Geoff explained that there are two different categories of Neuros; they could sell me both that afternoon, but a licensed doctor was required to install the more advanced version.

The Neuro Helm (TM) is non-invasive and usually set up by users' beds. You lie on your back and pull the Neuro, which resembles a shiny motorcycle helmet with cords sticking out the top, onto your head. Your face is uncovered. Geoff helped me to pull the display model over my skull. The inside of the helmet is covered in what feels like cool gel pads. It was a little heavy while standing up, but otherwise quite comfortable.

The Neuro Air (TM) is a thin little device, maybe half the length of my thumb, with a small protrusion in the middle where a cord or disc can be plugged in. A doctor inserts the device under the surface of the skin at the back of your neck, leaving the edge of the protrusion exposed to the air. Geoff tells me not to worry: the design is waterproof to 10 meters, so you can still shower and swim and get caught in a storm without worrying that you'll damage the technology (or yourself).

The advantage of the Neuro Air is that you can play and record Neuro experiences wherever you are – you don't have to be tethered to the Neuro Helm to access your system. But I was a beginner who wasn't going to let an unknown entity get inserted into my neck, so the Neuro Helm was the right choice for me.

At the time of writing this article, the Neuro Helm will set you back a tidy $1,100 AU. The Neuro Air is significantly more expensive at $1,950, plus whatever your doctor charges for the installation. Still, these prices have already come down a lot since launch, and are likely to drop further as Neuros saturate the market.

SETTING UP

I propped my new Neuro Helm on a stool beside my bed. It needs to be plugged into power to work, and there's an optional cord to plug it into a wired internet connection. Wireless works fine for the average user, but the wired connection is faster. As my Neuro already required one cord and I had a modem set up in the bedroom, I plugged the network cord into the top of the helmet as well.

After settling on the bed with the Neuro snug over my head, I switched it on via a button over my right ear. It took a few heartbeats to boot up, shown by a series of tiny green lights that flashed to life just above my eyebrows. Then there was the familiar Neuro synth-chime (I promise you, if you're a hearing person who has been at all active in the world in the last twelve months, you will have heard this radiating out from *somewhere*), and I was plunged into momentary darkness.

The single second between the darkness and the menu loading was one of the longest of my life. It was as if I had been plunged into a sensory deprivation tank.

As if I had died.

I saw nothing, heard nothing (really *nothing*, not even my own breath), smelt nothing, tasted nothing. For the first time, I realised that my own mouth had a taste, and that it was *missing*. I could still feel the cotton bed covers under my fingers, dimly, but it was like the sensation of touch had been dialled down to half. The main Neuro menu had loaded, bright and welcoming, but I fumbled with the button on my helmet and switched it to 'off'. To my great relief, all the sensations of the world returned almost instantly.

After getting up for a calming drink of water, I tried the Neuro again. This time, with a better understanding of what to expect, I was shocked to find I loved it. Any minor aches or tension in my body vanished. I felt liberated from my body in a way that I had only felt before in my dreams. I spent a few minutes simply sitting in that half-weightless nothing, not focusing on the menu at all.

As an aside, for those who would not enjoy this, I now know that there is an option to retain your sensations (minus your real-life visuals) while you browse the main menu. You can adjust this from the 'burger' sub-menu (the one with the three horizontal lines) as soon as the main menu loads — select the 'Experience Settings' option and make your adjustments.

Unlike other similar menus you may have tried in the past, Neuro menus do not need to be controlled with your eye movements. Simply shift your focus to wherever feels natural and select items with your intention (as a beginner, I visualised clicking something with an imaginary finger). While this can be initially disorienting, I was surprised at how quickly this type of navigation felt natural.

INTRODUCTORY EXPERIENCES

The first experiences offered to me on the main menu were grouped under 'Recommended for new users,' which sounded exactly like the kind of cautious start I wanted. The image thumbnails suggested a sunny seaside town, a hot spring, a tropical beach, or a cosy log fire. With any anxious anticipation artificially dulled, I went ahead and selected the tropical beach scene.

Immediately, my sensations started to shift, like falling gently out of a dream. The first thing I noticed was the heat: the sun radiating down, the warm breeze ruffling my shirt, the hot sand between my toes. The light was so much brighter, reflecting off the dunes and waves, than in my bedroom, but my new eyes were almost used to it. Then my new body – the body I was borrowing, the body of the woman who originally recorded that experience – started to move, and I was overwhelmed by the difference between our physical realities. How her longer, athletic legs travelled with such fluidity down the beach. How her smaller breasts didn't bounce as we walked. The sensation of where her shoulders and nose sat in space. And she was so happy, so content. I could feel it through her whole body, her whole mind.

She climbed onto a padded, plastic recliner so that her top half was shaded and her legs were still hot in the sun. We looked up into the gently waving palm fronds. We looked out where small children were playing joyfully in the shallows. A bartender handed her a strawberry-coloured cocktail, and the glass was chilled in our long fingers. Everything smelt of warm, fresh salt air. When she lifted the drink to our lips, her hands smelt of coconut.

I stayed in that experience for its full fifty-four minutes. At that point, it kicked me out smoothly, back to the weightless nothing of the main menu. It had felt like fifteen minutes. I had been in paradise, and although objectively, nothing had *happened*, I was alarmed by how much my entire waking worldview seemed to have shifted.

My bedroom was getting dark, and a little cold. I switched on the light and the heater, ate a small dinner with my husband, and then replayed the same beach experience once more later that night.

A REASSURANCE

What happens if there's a fire? I wondered, before I had my first experience. *Would I hear the alarm? What if I'm suddenly in pain, in danger, and my body can't tell me because I'm hooked into the Neuro?*

Your Neuro is programmed to notice any sufficiently loud alarm and interrupt your experience. The same applies to any significant, unexpected pain. There are stories of parents getting booted back to reality because their toddler started chewing on their motionless toes.

Personally, I have had an experience interrupted because my cat leapt onto my stomach too hard.

AIDEN WADE

"I've been doing this for a little over two years now," says Aiden, who earns about a quarter of his annual income from creating and uploading Neuro experiences. As opposed to typical Neuro content creators, for whom it's usually a matter of pride to leave their content as raw as possible, Aiden's experiences are a combination of unedited recordings and highly designed creations mixed into the same file. All of Aiden's nightly dreams are recorded via his Neuro Air, and about every four to six months he dreams a large chunk of a full-length new stage musical.

"Being able to record those dreams has been one of the most satisfying things in my life," he says. "I used to have them every so often before Neuros existed, and I would wake up with the knowledge that my brain had created these amazing, complex melodies, most of which I forgot within twenty minutes of waking. Now I can go back and re-experience them, and lots of other people can enjoy them, too."

Wherever his musical dreams cut out mid-song, seem to skip scenes, or otherwise don't provide a full stage musical experience, Aiden fills in the gaps with his imagination. This adds an extra layer of surrealism to his musicals, which can cut suddenly between a full-colour dreamscape and entirely black visuals. In these consciously added black parts, it feels a little like your eyes are closed and Aiden is telling you a story. Your brain still understands where the characters are moving in space, and what they're saying or singing, like replaying a song inside your head. You're imagining what Aiden is imagining, rather than having his dreams recreated in your brain. Sometimes his musicals can switch between these two methods of delivery multiple times within the span of a few minutes.

"It's not for everyone, of course," Aiden acknowledges. "But nothing is. It obviously works well enough for my 380,000 subscribers."

One of the most interesting things about Aiden's musicals, to me, is that Aiden can't read or write sheet music. When I ask him whether he'd ever want to see his musicals on a physical stage, he grins: "Of course, if someone wanted to spend the money producing them. I'm unlikely to have that kind of money any time soon. And they'd need some adaptation: I smooth some things out with my editing and additions, but to the Neuro audience, the dream logic can be more of a feature than a bug. In real life, audiences don't want to sit through two hours of dream surrealism."

If you're keen to try out one of Aiden's dream musicals, I would recommend starting with 'Amazing Light', which has a soaring score and is set in a popular wig shop at the end of the world. Searching 'Aiden Wade' on your Neuro should bring up his experience channel.

A CONVERSATION OVER WINE

Soon after I had started using my Neuro in earnest, one of my best friends – I'll call her Skye – contacted me, saying: "Thank God, I've been wanting to talk to you about something, but until you tried the Neuro I wasn't sure you'd understand."

Skye has been a big fan of actress and personality Leonie Diamond for at least half a decade now. Over a nice rich Shiraz, Skye told me that she'd tried Leonie's recent 'sex tape' (apparently, everyone is still calling them that) on her Neuro and that this had led to a not-insignificant identity crisis.

"I thought Leonie would have recorded the experience," said Skye. "I'd just assumed. But it wasn't her point of view at all." In fact, the sex tape was recorded by Leonie's husband, Ashton Diamond, which (given the general audience for these things) is not really a surprise. But Skye's reaction certainly surprised her.

"I found it absolutely addictive. I'd never wanted to be a man before, but suddenly – it felt so good to be Ashton. So perfect." Skye couldn't tell if these new thoughts were because of Leonie, or just that particular Neuro experience, or something deeper. Her own body, devoid of Ashton's parts, had begun to feel misshapen and wrong.

By the time we'd polished off the bottle of wine, Skye said, "I'm going to force myself not to play that experience for two whole months. After that, I should better understand what's going on."

I assured her that I would support her no matter what.

(Months later, Skye has decided that she doesn't feel the need to be a man in her real life. Still, it can be satisfying to play one on the Neuro.)

ANDREA REDA

Andrea is the creator of that very first tropical beach experience I chose that first day. I meet her one Saturday morning in a fashionable breakfast-cafe-slash-smoothie-bar with rose gold animal heads protruding from the walls. Her skin practically glows next to her red patterned sundress. It is strange to see her and think: *I know what it was like to be you for fifty-four minutes.*

"I definitely have one of the best jobs in the world," says Andrea. "I'm not denying that at all. I get to go to wonderful, beautiful places and record myself having a fabulous time in them." She sips her thick green smoothie; there is probably kale in it. "But people think there's no effort involved, that I'm just on holidays all the time. That's not true. I have to keep myself in top physical and mental condition to create the kind of experiences I do. And I have to keep my mind almost totally clear while I'm recording. No one wants to play an escapist experience and then have the thought, 'I have to remember to check out at 10:00 AM tomorrow' interrupt it. That takes practice."

I ask her which experience was her favourite to record. "Oh, there are so many amazing ones. I don't think I have a favourite. Off the top of my head..." She counts on her fingers. "Snorkelling in Fiji. Throngs of brightly coloured fish swim around you like you belong there; they'll eat bread from your fingers. Sailing into Antarctica. Skiing in New Zealand. Seeing the northern lights shimmer above me in Norway."

Andrea's excitement is infectious. I'd played her northern lights experience before, and remembered being rugged up in a parka two inches thick, watching the magical lights with our arm around a sleepy husky, the other hand clutching a mug of steaming green tea. It had gotten me back to drinking green tea in the mornings.

What does she do when she's not working? "Well, for fun I like to read, play piano and go horse riding. But I'm mostly working on a book these days. I know this charmed life I have can't last forever. Someday, I'm going to get too old or lose a leg or become mentally ill and people aren't going to want to play those experiences like they do right now. So I need something else to fall back on."

Andrea's book is called *Sharing My Spirit* and is a memoir of her work travelling the globe to bring holiday experiences to others, especially the 'backstage' elements that most of her fans don't already know. It's expected for publication summer next year with Foxgrove Press.

HARRIET LIM

Dr Harriet Lim is a general practitioner with East Glenferrie Medical Clinic. About five months prior to our interview, Dr Lim had a Neuro Helm installed above her office's examination table to better understand how patients were feeling.

"Truly, it's been revolutionary," Dr Lim tells me. "I was first introduced to the Neuro by my cousin. He'd installed it for recreational use, but he had a friend send him a recording of a sunset – which was beautiful – where my cousin thought: my friend seems to feel terrible. Is this normal? My cousin tried the recording on me to check, and it was only about a minute long, but I was able to say: no, this is definitely not normal. Your friend needs medical attention. In fact, he had a severe case of Giardia, an intestinal parasite, and needed antibiotics."

Since then, Dr Lim has been using the Neuro to get a clearer picture of her patients' bodies and minds, usually for specific ailments, but occasionally as a general check-up.

"The most shocking thing to me," says Dr Lim, "is how much I used to rely on patients performing their pain to me. Now I can have a patient come in – they seem calm, they seem perfectly lucid – and I take a two-minute snapshot of their bodies with the Neuro and experience it for myself... They can be in terrible pain. Pain that I wouldn't be walking around with, pain that would have me in tears. And then I can diagnose or make decisions with that patient based on their actual experience of their body."

Dr Lim has had some patients who thought they were fine, and then when she has experienced their Neuro recordings there has been something obviously wrong. "Previously, it would have been very hard to help these people, who would not have told me anything was out of the ordinary. But some of them, I can tell right away: they need glasses, or they're having some trouble breathing, or they have pain in their hands that I now know feels like arthritis. You can know how something is 'supposed' to feel from a textbook, but it's different to briefly understand how it feels for yourself. It makes me a better doctor."

There have also been some other surprises for Dr Lim. "Sometimes the Neuro will tell me: 'The experience you are trying to play is not fully compatible with your brain. Would you like to experience an approximation?' And this in itself tells me, this person's brain works a bit different to my own. Usually they have a neuro-divergence like ADHD or autism, which sometimes they know but sometimes they don't, or they could have a mental illness, or occasionally it can mean some kind of brain damage. In the case of neuro-divergence it can be incredibly validating to the patient, who might have sensed that they are operating at a slightly different wavelength than the rest of the world, to know that there is a medical reason. I had a father bring in a teenage girl – they were fighting often, verbally – and that message on the Neuro was the trigger to get her an autism diagnosis. Before that, they had no idea. And they purchased a Neuro, so he could experience an approximation of how she goes through the world. How so much that is easy for him is uncomfortable or painful for her, and how much anxiety she experiences on a day-to-day basis. It has completely changed their relationship."

I ask Dr Lim about the adoption of Neuros throughout the wider medical community. "They are certainly becoming more common," she said. "Just in the past couple of months, they are becoming more mainstream, considered more necessary. I have multiple colleagues who use them in their surgeries now. And I believe there is at least one in the majority of large hospitals in the country. I think those numbers will keep going up for a while."

BEN KOPIN

Ben's channel is a food channel, but he explains to me that there are lots of different sub-genres of food channels: "There are people who play these experiences because they want to feel full, and there are people who want to have the sense of eating with a group of people. There are also experiences for people who just really love french fries, for example, and they just want to eat french fries for 40 minutes. My channel isn't really any of those things. My channel is about tasting a little of a lot of food. So I make experiences like '10 Japanese dishes you probably haven't tried before' or 'Let's eat most of this restaurant's menu together'. Usually, I just eat a couple of bites of whatever I'm trying. I might come back multiple nights or weeks in a row. It gets expensive, but my subscribers love it. They cover my restaurant bills. Or sometimes the restaurants will sponsor me, because my experiences can really boost their popularity."

Although Ben's channel deals exclusively with food, his channel is one of a sub-genre of Neuro experiences that are widely referred to as 'samplers'. For these experiences, creators cut together a variety of different moments to create a package like, 'Feeling 20 different types of fabric' or 'Drinking coffee in cafes all around the world'. Part of the appeal of these rapid-fire packages is the contrast of one section of the experience versus the next. Playing the experience might have you sweating in Vanuatu for one minute, and then rugged up in Canada a minute later.

JOSH SHARMA

Josh makes me tea with milk and one sugar. We both take it the same way, but our cups don't match: his is a bright pattern of green and orange squares, and mine a detailed painting of leaping wolves. Above our heads, there are the occasional thumps of his teenage daughter clattering around in her room.

"That was her mug," he says, gesturing to the wolves. I am visiting to talk about his late wife, who passed away about three months ago. I hold the cup a little more carefully.

"We had to write to Knott," said Josh, "for special permission." (Knott Inc. are the technology company that created the Neuros.) "I don't think more than a hundred people have gotten it. Though, of course... I hope they keep expanding and offering it to more. It made such a difference to Louisa. Knowing that she didn't suffer. That she was happy, in her last moments."

The difference for Louisa, he explains to me, is that they knew in advance that she was terminal, and approximately how long she had left. They had time to prepare. And some of that time was used to contact Knott to make appropriate arrangements.

"On her last day," says Josh, who is quiet but steady, "a representative from Knott arrived with a special type of Neuro. The normal models, you can't bypass the part that shuts things down if it senses you're in danger. Not even with Knott permissions. So they bring this special model, it's a different colour, like medical blue. And the person from Knott, they unlock it. We say all our goodbyes. And then when we're ready, they put it on her head. It's pre-programmed with all the experiences she's chosen. Skiing and parasailing and eating toffee ice cream. And I hold her hand the whole time, even though she can't feel it. She doesn't feel anything, even when her heart stops. In her head, she's still skiing down that slope in Switzerland, right until the very end."

Tears have tracked down both our cheeks by then, but you can't tell by Josh's voice. We sip our tea. "I hope I get to go out that way," says Josh. "I hope a lot of people do."

KATRINA WILLIAMS-ONLY

Katrina, a polished middle-aged woman with a glamorous fringe and tailored jacket, describes her job at Knott as, "Keeping Neuro users safe."

"I'm very passionate about what Neuros make possible," Katrina tells me over video conferencing. "Neuros are all about equality of experience: if one person can do something and record it, billions of other people around the planet can experience that, too. It's an empathy revolution. You can literally walk in someone else's shoes. 99% of what Neuros offer is so, so positive. But of course, on any user-based platform, there's that 1% that we potentially need to protect users from. And distinguishing that 1%, and deciding how we manage it, that can be a very fine line, but we do our best."

I mention my recent meeting with Josh Sharma, and how his wife passed away while wearing Neuro technology.

She nodded. "Oh yes, so that's an example of something we would never want to happen to our normal users. We would never want Neuros to keep running if users were in any significant pain or danger. But there are special exceptions. Similarly, what happens to users with chronic pain? We don't want to block them from using our product because their baseline level of pain is high. So in that case, we ask for signed declarations from those users' doctors, and we take a measurement of what a 'normal' level of pain or distress is for that patient, and adjust the settings of their Neuro accordingly."

I hadn't even thought of that before she mentioned it. "So that's for playing those experiences," I say, thinking of people I've known who have been very unwell. "What about if users in pain want to record experiences, too?"

"Yes, good question. That was one of Knott's first social concerns when developing this technology. Because part of the human experience is being in pain, but do we want to actively help people to feel that pain? What are our responsibilities there? Is our responsibility to minimise users' pain when they're in an experience, or is our responsibility to accurately portray the awfulness of an experience, if it is awful? We don't want people to think that experiences are harmless or insignificant when that isn't the case at all."

Katrina pauses for a moment here, and then continues. "What we currently do with the Neuros, and it's not a perfect solution, but I think it's the best one we've got, is that we let users set their own pain settings, both globally and for individual experiences. So they can set them from no pain at all, all the way up to moderate pain. We don't allow anything more than moderate pain on our devices. And for videos with any pain or discomfort, we warn users about that beforehand so they can adjust their settings, or so they understand that this experience is actually causing the person recording it much more pain in real life. It's very important to us that they understand that."

"Of course," Katrina adds, "I'm talking about legal activities only. We don't allow experiences involving illegal activities on our platform. Our algorithm usually catches them before they even go live, but we also have a team of dedicated staff to identify and remove them, and users can also flag experiences as a last resort."

I ask Katrina if there are a lot of people uploading illegal activity to the Neuro library. "No, it's a tiny percentage of experiences. We share them with the police, so really, it's a very stupid move for anyone to make."

On the topic of legality, I asked her about copyright on the platform. "That's an interesting one, because the Neuro is a completely new way of capturing and conveying someone's experience of the world. There were multiple court cases soon after it launched. Using some music in a video without permission is illegal, but displaying a painting in the background of an experience without permission is not. And ultimately, there are nuances like whether a Neuro experience is more manufactured or not, but the rulings were that a Neuro experience is more like that photograph: someone is going about their life and that painting – or song, or animation – is in the background, and it's legal to include it without violating copyright."

In terms of keeping Neuro users safe, Katrina explains that Knott's two other major concerns were addiction and mental illness.

"Addictions can be to good experiences – eating delicious food, dancing in a club, having sex – or they can be to experiences with a lot of adrenaline involved, or even negative experiences, although that's much more rare. We don't want to nanny our users too much, but there are settings you can change on your Neuro so that you're not playing a particular experience or type of experience too often. And we do have a global setting, for all users, that we control from Knott headquarters. That global setting prevents users from spending more than 12 hours a day actively playing Neuro experiences from one device. Some people will say that's far too lenient or far too strict, but that's the number we're using at the moment."

When speaking about mental illness, Katrina clasps her hands tightly on the other side of the screen. "The tricky thing about mental illness," she says, "is that we don't want to stop users with mental illness from recording and sharing their experiences, obviously, but we know that the human brain is tremendously plastic. So there is this real concern, for instance, that duplicating the experiences of clinically anxious users too many times for people who don't have clinical anxiety, their brains could get used to that anxious state – that essentially, we could trigger mental illness in users by simulating that experience. For these kinds of experiences that we advise users to limit their consumption of, we currently display a warning at the start of each experience, and we also present users with the option of only playing the visual and audio parts of those experiences, so they can still enjoy a lot of the content without the risk."

Given the brain's plasticity, I ask Katrina whether playing the experiences of non-depressed people might be able to help their users with depression, for example.

"There's research going into that sort of thing right now, actually," she tells me. "And we're hopeful that it might help in some cases. But truly, in relation to depression, I don't think it will work for a lot of people. That doesn't mean that depressed users can't enjoy and benefit from Neuro content, but severe depression can be so complex and varied, and the Neuro has its limitations."

IN CONCLUSION

It's been a very eventful four months. I've developed a strong appreciation of my Neuro, and I don't think I'll be getting rid of it any time soon. I've been continually surprised by how enriching Neuro experiences can be, and I'll be following the expanding applications of Neuros in society with great interest.

WHEN THE ICE COMES IN

I'm curled up in the middle of the carpet, away from the windows where the cold is worst. I am wearing two beanies, two scarves around my face, several layers including a snow jacket, and four or five blankets, but I am still so cold. The gas, electricity and phone signals are out. The gas, electricity and phone signals are out for everyone.

The curtains are drawn to keep what little heat remains inside, but I know exactly what the view looks like: snow drifts so high I could almost step onto them from my second-storey apartment. But I don't think I'm going anywhere. I'm so cold I can barely move. And where would I go?

This apartment block is not built for snow. There has never been snow here before. Bushfires — those we know how to deal with. I picture an inferno outside, capturing the trees and igniting them into fiery beacons. The church outside, smoking and smouldering brick by brick. *Fire, fire everywhere and not a flame to flick.*

Wait. The matches in the cupboard are long gone, of course, but didn't I drop a pack beside the stove a few months ago?

Didn't I? I think so. It has to be worth a check.

I uncurl myself from the blanket nest, slowly, stiffly. Clumsy because my hands are numb. I force myself to stagger to the kitchen, to shove the oven to the side with my elbow.

There, towards the back. A box of matches. Oh my god.

I kneel and stretch my arm awkwardly into the gap I've made beside the oven. It hurts my shoulder, but who cares? When my gloved hand makes contact with the box I know from sight, rather than touch, but I nudge it closer to me, closer...

There. I grasp the box between my clawed fingers and drop it into my lap. It rattles like maracas. Mine. Matches. What can I do with matches?

There isn't any wood in this fucking apartment. I had a single wooden chair that I threw onto the bonfire down the road, the one flaming in the middle of the street maybe twenty days ago when no-one thought things could get any worse. Why did I do that? It had seemed a good idea at the time...

I already burned the lantern oil. And the kitchen oil. The candles burnt out days ago. My books the day before yesterday. What else can I fucking burn?

I'm so cold. Maybe if I was a little warmer I could think better.

I fumble with the matchbox until I can push out the drawer with my forefinger. Count the matches inside: nine, two burnt and seven unburnt. Seven's okay. Seven's enough that I can strike one just to feel the heat. So I can thaw my hands a little. So I can think a little straighter.

The match finally lights on my eighth try. The flame hisses to life and I cup my free hand around the back of it, worshipping this drop of fire. And then it's not a drop anymore: there are legs and hips and arms and hair; the flame has morphed into the shape of a woman, no taller than my thumb.

"Hello," she says. Her voice sounds like water sizzling as it hits a gas burner.

"Hello," I croak.

"You need to put me somewhere, if you want me to last," she says. "You have those..."

But the flame hits the top of my fingers, and flickers, and goes out.

Another match. With as much panic as I can salvage in these temperatures, I fumble with the matchbox until I have another lit.

When the flame twists into her shape again I want to sing. "Crayons will burn up to half an hour in an emergency," she says. "Go. Go now."

With the match pinched carefully between my fingers, I struggle towards the hallway cupboard. There's a plastic crate in there where I kept toys for my niece and nephew... And down the bottom, under the cars and construction blocks, some crayons.

The second match has gone out, of course, because I wasn't quick enough. I empty the crayons out onto the floor: only two are left — apparently the kids don't use a lot of white or beige. I scoop them up with shaking hands and return to the living room.

I make another nest with all my blankets, on the couch this time as there's a film of ice across the carpet. I wrap myself up as best I can. I light the match, and then the beige crayon. A stronger flame shoots up from the crayon's tip, and there's the woman again, now the size of my forefinger. I hold the crayon just on top of my chest.

"Thank you," I say.

"Thank you for giving me a home."

I stare at her body floating in the flames. If I wasn't so cold, so exhausted, I'm sure I'd be laughing or crying by now.

"Why are you here?" I ask.

"To see you," she says. And that's more than good enough for me.

For as long as the crayon burns I am fixated on her, mesmerized, delirious. She is so beautiful, like a goddess, a genie, a djinn. I do not ask her what she is. I tell her everything, and she says I have had a good life, and that is true.

When the crayon burns out the cold rushes back in, and now it is properly dark, and my nose and hands, which were starting to hurt with the glorious pain of thawing out next to her warmth, turn icy and numb again. Tiny icicles form on my eyelashes. It is too much to bear.

I light the second crayon, and this time she tells me stories, the most wonderful stories I have ever heard. Stories of blooming deserts and families of phoenixes and shining palaces with towers that brush the stars. Stories of fire-eaters and fire-breathers and festivals a hundred nights long, where the sun never rises and everything is firelight and hot and good. Anywhere there is fire, she has been, and she can go.

When I light the fifth match she says, "Careful, you have no more crayons to burn."

When I light the sixth match I say, "I love you."

When I light the seventh match I just stare at her in silence, and that is enough.

"You need to watch out," she says. "Your hand is tilting. I'm getting very close to your blankets, and they're highly flammable. Stop."

"I don't want to be cold anymore," I say.

And then she's all over me, and I'm not cold, not ever again.

SMOL ANIMAUX

Prior to Smol Animaux, I was deep in one of the most miserable times of my life: pregnant, living alone, and in lockdown. When I'd decided to keep the baby I'd expected my family to visit often, to be able to sit in cafés with friends every week, to have support and community. Instead, the government safety rules had dictated no guests, no gatherings, and had limited leaving the house to little more than one hour a day.

Zoom calls can't hold you after you've emptied your breakfast into the toilet for the sixth day in a row. Zoom calls can't fetch you pistachio ice cream when you have an overwhelming craving at bedtime.

When I was inside twenty-three hours a day for weeks on end, I discovered that I could walk from one end of my apartment to the other with twelve steps. It was high winter, the middle of July, and I had the heater on almost constantly but didn't always feel warm, even with a blanket and beanie on. Usually the baby squirming around inside me was the only human contact I had all day.

One afternoon when the sun was brighter and the sky was mostly blue and bare, I was leaning on my balcony with a capsule coffee when I heard my neighbour's sliding door open. A girl stepped out – Violet – I'd met her briefly a couple of times before, but not since the pandemic started. I was lousy at guessing ages, but she was probably in her late teens, with a cropped neon orange hoodie and a can of highlighter-pink energy drink. When she stepped up to the fence that split the balcony between our properties, it came up to just below her eyes.

"Hey neighbour," she said, and I heard the top of the energy drink pop open. She raised it over her head in a kind of 'cheers'. I raised my coffee in return.

We spoke for a good twenty minutes, which was the longest I'd talked to anyone in person for weeks. Safety-wise, it wasn't the most sensible thing in the world, but we weren't technically breaking any rules, and I figured if one person in our apartment block got sick we probably all would, anyway.

Violet was going to be living there with her dad for the next several months, but he was hardly ever home. He must have some kind of exemption. He was high up somewhere in the company that made Smol Animaux, and that seemed to be the primary thing that she cared to discuss.

Had I heard of Smol Animaux before?

I hadn't.

Did I like animals?

Loved them, but didn't have any right now.

Violet had pulled a plastic chair up to the fence by that point and was standing on it, so I could see her caffeinated grin when she said, "Perfect. There are a couple of example systems just inside. Life's shit for everyone right now, but especially if you're living alone. I'll set one up for you for free."

Several minutes later she had hopped over the balcony fence with a tote bag, fixed me a fizzy drink in my kitchen that looked like Berocca, and was busy installing a new A5-sized device next to my TV. It looked a bit like a modem with a touchscreen covering the front.

Violet finished tapping a code into the screen. "What kind of animals do you like? Pugs? King Charles Spaniels? Tabby cats?"

I sipped my orange drink while I considered. Apparently the device could handle anything the size of a Corgi or smaller. Without too much thought I settled on a Pomeranian and a Siamese, and Violet nodded and made some more adjustments to the device.

"So how does this work?" I asked. "Is it like holograms or something? Augmented reality? Do I need special glasses?"

She chuckled, throaty and deep. "No glasses. But yeah, it's like advanced AR. You'll see the animals moving around your apartment, even though they're not really there. You'll feel them, too."

I must have looked truly sceptical then, because her smile became even cockier. "Give it a minute."

"But how– What's the interface?"

Victoria gestured towards my empty glass. "Nanobots."

I stared at the orange residue, one hand moving protectively over my belly. Was she joking? A wash of cold dread rippled through my body.

Violet activated the device. Before I could ask any more questions my apartment was suddenly filled with life. A fluffy fox-coloured Pomeranian stood before me, tapping its feet in happiness on my wooden floor. A sleek Siamese cat stretched on my couch cushions, bottom in the air and yawning wide. The Pomeranian's shiny dark eyes and the Siamese's clear blue ones gazed at me with love, and despite my reservations I instantly loved them, too.

It's not an exaggeration to say that those imaginary animals saved my life. When I buried my hands in their plush fur, my brain told me they felt soft and silky. When I lay on the couch I felt their warmth on my chest, above the roundness of the baby, or the weight of them curled on my lap. They never needed to eat, or excrete waste, or go to the vet. They had permanent good moods. I could hear the purr of the cat and the occasional excited yip of the dog, even if no-one else ever could. Just because they weren't real, that didn't stop them from calming me. It didn't stop them from making me smile, or from providing me with comfort and companionship when I had no-one else.

It was clear why Violet's father was so invested in this technology. My new animals would never grow old, or die, or need a kennel when I went on holiday. They functioned perfectly within a 200-metre radius of the device, so even people with far larger homes than mine would be able to maintain the illusion seamlessly. By upgrading my membership I could get more pets; more than two in number, but also a wider variety of species, and also fantastical variants like a lavender-coloured dachshund or a cat with little bat wings. If it was corgi-sized or smaller, nothing was impossible.

My Smol Animaux continued to comfort me after the baby came home. His name was Theo, and I loved him intensely, but the first couple of months were so exhausting that I felt like a shell of myself. He seemed to cry constantly, which made my heart hurt for him but also for me, and sometimes he had trouble latching to feed. Everything was so hard. When I collapsed after putting him in the bassinet, it was a small blessing to feel the Pomeranian lick my fingers. To have the Siamese wind around my ankles while I sat almost in tears. We were still in lockdown. For those first couple of months, barring a couple of doctor's visits, some brief chats with neighbours, and the occasional walk around the block, I had no other company.

At the two-month mark, when the baby's immune system was more tolerant of visitors, Violet jumped the fence between our balconies and started babysitting for me a couple of times per week. Mostly, I would use this time to sleep. I paid her a nominal fee in cash, and everyone was happy.

This went on for several weeks, until Violet announced that her dad would be moving out of the building. She seemed apologetic about it, but they'd be living too far away for her to continue babysitting for me, regardless of the lockdown. I was polite about this, of course, but my stomach felt like it had dropped into my feet. I was barely keeping my head above water as it was.

But despite my worries, life with Theo seemed to be improving on its own. The apartment next door may have emptied, but I was finally sleeping through the night a lot more. My baby had grown calmer, more content. He latched more reliably, although he didn't seem to be drinking very much. Little rivulets of milk ran down my stomach and left wet marks on my t-shirts. I would've been more concerned if he wasn't still plump and smiling up at me, eyes bright.

Twenty minutes before Theo's four-month doctor's appointment, I strapped him into his rear-facing car seat on the driver's side. During previous car trips to the doctor he had screamed and cried, but this time he just gurgled a little as I strapped him in, and I gave him a quick kiss on the forehead, thinking this time would be better.

He was quiet for the whole ride.

At the doctor's car park, I climbed out and just gawked through the car's backseat window. Theo was gone. I blinked rapidly, hoping that would make him reappear. It didn't. My panic spiked astronomically and I thrust my hands into the car seat, as if he'd become invisible. He hadn't fallen out onto the floor of the car. He wasn't anywhere at all.

My vision was spinning. I forced myself back into the driver's seat and to take deep breaths. If Theo definitely wasn't here, then he must be back at my apartment. I thought I'd remembered strapping him in earlier, but obviously I hadn't. Maybe he was lying on the edge of my apartment's numbered car park, next to the spray-painted number five.

It normally took ten minutes to drive back home, but this time I made it in seven. I scrambled out of my seat, heart in my mouth.

There was Theo, strapped snugly into his baby seat in the back of my car, where I'd left him. He looked perfectly fine.

I was losing my mind. I knelt beside him on the bitumen and wept.

I debated whether to still go to the doctor's appointment. We'd be ten minutes late. I was a mess, but so were many new mothers. I took several deep breaths. I could do it. We had better go.

I strapped myself back in and drove back to the doctor, much more carefully this time.

At the doctor's, Theo was gone again.

My panic had faded somewhat. Now I just felt heavy, with chest pains, like I was drowning.

I took myself back home one last time, releasing Theo mechanically and carrying him upstairs in his car seat like I was moving through treacle. The Pomeranian and Siamese greeted me at the door. I bent down to pat each of them, then moved to the Smol Animaux device next to the TV.

Once I woke up the little screen, underneath the rows for the dog and the cat was a third row without a name, with a tiny lock icon next to it. All of the remaining warmth left my body.

I looked down at them: the Pomerian, the Siamese, and Theo in his car seat. Smaller than corgi-sized animals, all of them.

All of them.

THE MOST POWERFUL WITCH IN WITCHVILLE

In the thickest part of the forest stretches a stone wall as tall as its tallest tree. Inside the wall is Witchville.

Witchville, which by its current population is truly more like a large town than a village, is enchanted to look like any adjacent patch of forest from the air. Living things may pass through this enchanted barrier, but foreign man-made things may not, so on rare occasions naked outsiders have been known to drop into the town, preceded by the brief fireworks display of their clothing incinerating at the vertical town line.

Down inside the wall, intricate buildings pack close together. Closest to the edge of town the structures are small and modest, but grow in size and grandeur as one approaches the centre, with the tallest towers clustering around the central square. Almost all of the architecture involves stone or dark wood in variants of black, grey, and purple, so that the town gives off the overwhelming impression of liquorice allsorts or a gothic gingerbread village brought to life.

Presently, it is the evening, so a great many candles, floating lanterns and candelabras light the streets and windows of Witchville. In the middle of the central square, a twelve-year-old girl with ruby red hair gets a copper-coloured '5th' ribbon pinned to her chest. Standing to either side of her, the other nine recipients of ribbons are all tired-looking adults.

But perhaps we are a little early. Let's skip ahead five years, to the next competition, and then about another five years after that. The ruby red-haired girl is twenty-two, and about to compete for the second time to be the most powerful witch in Witchville.

#

SATURDAY

The girl's name is Nicolette Elliesdaugh, but it has been shortened to Coal for much of the girl's life, which was her idea, after all. It is Saturday morning, two days before the competition. Her early morning routine is always the same:

It starts with shooting electricity from her palms into a heavily-singed boxing bag, then hissing another spell to soothe those electrical burns, and slathering on some extra salve for good measure.

She breathes life into the slack body of a wax sparrow and sends it to swoop through the town while she jogs on a treadmill, seeing the town waking up directly through its eyes.

She serves herself up another problem that the town has or could have and crafts as many plans to solve it as she can manage in a second fifteen minutes.

By this time her palms have healed completely, and she performs a series of tricks on her modified floating broom in the relative confines of her basement bedroom. Her broom has a bike seat and bike handles screwed into the wood. Many residents in Witchville travel on floating pushbikes, but Coal prefers the smaller footprint and easier manoeuvrability of her modified broom.

Finally, she spends five minutes mentally scanning her whole body for imperfections or sickness, magically reduces some swelling that has flared in her left elbow, and then takes the best version of herself upstairs for breakfast.

Near the top of their house, which is tall and thin with a room per floor, both her parents are pottering in the kitchen. They'd initially connected through a shared love of wax magic, and the kitchen table is still full of wax masks and wax bumblebees, plus Genevieve's marshmallow toast and an open novel dotted with a single breadcrumb. Genevieve, whose default uniform is a suit with silver arrow cufflinks, uses the wax masks to transform herself in her acting career.

Saika stirs something sweet and meaty on the burner. Her dresses are all floaty hedge-witch, layers weighted down with sewn gemstones and jewels. She specialises in wax insects. When she whispers phrases to the wax bumblebees on the table, they'll fly off to land in the ears of townspeople and slip the phrase into their heads, and the only indication it didn't start there might be a wax smear on the floor or extra wax on their ear.

After she's eaten her fill of Saika's honey-dipped jackalope, Coal heads off to tutor some of the younger girls in town in the basics of magic. If they have the capacity for magic, even the slowest ones manage to perform some rudimentary magic within a couple of months.

In the evening she flies up to Porsha's mansion on the hill, one of the few houses in Witchville that still has a sizeable garden despite its relative centrality. Porsha won the competition ten years ago, when Coal placed fifth, and has easily retained her position since then. Porsha has been Coal's mentor since Coal was eighteen, and Coal's lover since Coal was twenty, the inevitable end of a long dance, although neither of them ever acknowledge a non-professional relationship. Coal's parents narrow their eyes and say, "She'll break your heart," but Coal only laughs. Coal is Porsha's Saturday evening visitor. Porsha has other visitors for all the other days, and Coal has no interest in competing with them. Their weekly meetings force her to push further, to have backup plans and then backup plans for those plans, as she can't tell Porsha what she actually intends to do to win. Porsha hears her second-best plans, her second-best thoughts and feelings. The first-best are reserved purely for the competition.

The autumn evening is slightly chilly, so Coal and Porsha take their rosehip and mint tea in Porsha's parlour with the curtains open to watch the town lights. They discuss the strengths and weaknesses of the other expected contestants. Coal describes shooting fireballs channelled through the broom's bike handles, which is really only the plan if the flesh starts peeling off her hands. Porsha warns her to be cautious; setting any part of the forest alight will automatically disqualify her from that round. Coal gets tired of deception and slips her hand into Porsha's shirt. Porsha waves her fingers to shut the mahogany curtains, and then Coal barely has to speak for the rest of the evening.

MONDAY

After the town's council has confirmed the final registration, the twenty-two competing witches are immediately thrust into their first challenge. Over the last few days, any sick or injured citizens that have been deemed non-urgent have had their healing delayed and have been collected this morning in the town square. Competing witches are randomly allocated with a sick or injured person and must heal them with accuracy and speed.

Coal draws a young witch with influenza. She knows immediately that this will be one of the hardest tasks as the virus isn't localised; it will be spread throughout her patient's body. She tries not to register the other patients, tries not to think about Porsha's huge advantage for this activity. Half the town have visited Porsha when they're unwell, joining the queue outside her house like they're seeking an audience with a queen. Coal focuses in on her patient's lacy white shirt and the voices of the council members.

When they're given permission, Coal shuts her eyes and wraps her hands over her patient's shoulders, quickly developing a mental map of the woman's inner body and then pinpointing one of the virus particles. She keeps a mental finger on that particle and extends her attention from there, sweeping the body in ever-expanding circles until she finally has all of them locked down. Finally, she can send an eliminating shockwave down through her own neck and through her hands, and she sees pulses behind her eyelids as she senses the virus particles break down and vanish from her patient.

When she opens her eyes her patient is sitting up straighter, and one of the council members has a hand against the young woman's forehead and is noting down a time. Around Coal most of her competitors are still working. Porsha is sitting on a stone fence nearby, soaking up the retreating sunlight like she's been there for ages. Three others have also finished; Coal recognises two of them as professional healers. After half an hour, four competitors have still been unsuccessful and are disqualified from the rest of the competition, and the council announces the scores.

Drusilla, one of the professional healers, has the highest score for this round. Porsha is second. Coal has the third highest score, not having been the third quickest, but having had a score boost from the difficulty level of her patient's illness.

Coal retrieves a coin of cockatrice jerky from her hip pocket. She finds Porsha's gaze and is about to deliver a playful wink, but Porsha winks first, and Coal certainly isn't going to *return* that. Instead, she contents herself with chewing on the cockatrice and stretching out her hands in preparation for the next round.

MONDAY EVENING

They activate the first wave of mechanical spiders half an hour before sunset. Coal and her seventeen other competitors have been given equal starting positions within the outskirts of the city. Coal keeps her eye on the town wall, bare feet on the ground and broom firmly tucked between her legs, until the city-wide horn sounds to signal that this round of the competition has begun. Her body sings with excitement, like a plucked violin string.

Coal leaps into the air and soars straight over the wall like a projectile. It doesn't take long to see her prey scuttle out of the forest, clean and sharp and eight-legged, the size of an average dog. They're fast and relatively intelligent, but the only thing that really matters is that they know who killed them.

Coal swoops down upon the first wave and thrusts out her palm. She has good aim by now; the lightning arcs out of her hand and hits a spider right in its abdomen. Sending the magic straight out of her flesh means that it's undiluted enough to extinguish the spider in one hit. It shudders, immediately collapsing into a heap of smoking and twisted metal. Her hand only hurts badly for a moment. She performs the accompanying healing spell within seconds, and then circles her broom around in a loop to attack the rest of the swarm.

By the time she has taken out five of them, some of the spiders have started to ascend the wall, digging their pointed legs into the gaps between the stones and amongst the vines. Coal shifts her focus to these spiders; if any make it down off the wall inside the town, it's illegal to continue hunting them, and killing them no longer counts towards a competitor's total. She flies along the outer wall horizontally, with the stones at her feet, and picks off the rising spiders as she glides. Sparks shoot off their shiny carapaces into the descending twilight.

Once she has eliminated all of the spiders in her immediate vicinity, Coal turns her attention to the horizon. What looks like a miniature fireworks show is erupting several hundred metres along the wall to her right; she shoots off along the inner wall to pick off any spiders that may have gotten past a slower witch.

Hair almost brushing against the town grass, she ends up shooting down three additional spiders from the inner wall, and then arcs back over to meet the second wave.

Each wave of the mechanical targets is larger and more concentrated, increasing the challenge, but also forcing the witches to directly compete for their kills within the same areas. By the third wave, Coal is flying amongst three other women. By the fourth, Porsha is impossible to miss: she's shooting electricity from a metal point that's been installed at the tip of her own modified broom. Porsha still has to shoot the spiders twice to knock them down, but she doesn't have to heal her hands between strikes. Still, Coal has more manoeuvrability. Coal drops the spider on the wall nearest Porsha. Porsha's amber eyes meet hers for a split second; they've both been lying to each other.

Coal is determined to use her agility to her advantage. She twists her neck, arms and hands around her body like rubber, spearing spiders with lightning from all angles. She locks her body on the broom with her thighs and flies hands-free, flashing magic from both hands like a mirror ball. She alights on the top of the wall and hits the spiders running down it like bowling practice.

It isn't until they sound the horn the second time that she allows herself to look at Porsha again. Then she can see it in the older woman's face: this round, Coal has won.

They eat a celebratory dinner: Coal, Genevieve, Saika, and Coal's best friend Rion. Six months ago, Rion had her hair and fingernails enchanted to grow in hot pink, and Coal can still pick her out of a crowd a hundred metres away.

"Bet you could've even taken it when you were seventeen," Rion says, dipping her sourdough bread in a mix of blood and gravy. "But no, no; you had to wait."

Coal snorts. "I would've probably come away second," she says, "and given away all my secrets." She sucks her knife clean and taps it twice against her nose. "Besides, there are still three rounds to go. Nothing's for granted."

Both of Coal's hands have been slathered with cooling cream inside awkward-looking medical gloves, and they still sting, but she's grateful there's no permanent damage.

Dessert is chocolate mousse laced with charisma-enchanted caramel rivulets. When they've all eaten their fill, Coal performs a dry run of tomorrow's presentation to the Council, and the whole height of the house echoes with clapping.

TUESDAY

The Council will hear thirteen presentations today, following the elimination of the bottom third of the contestants from Monday evening's spider hunt. Coal's will have no pictures, no slides, no illusions. This is a gamble, but she wants the six council members to be looking at her face, not at any distractions.

They bring the contestants in one at a time. In the meantime, Coal's alone in the cosy waiting room outside the council chambers, but she can sense traces of the last few contestants lingering inside the space. Porsha was here: her pale violet essence leaving cloudy smears in the air for those who knew what to look for. Coal reaches out and runs her fingers through the smear: confidence, intelligence, a little irritation. On the other side of the room, she suspects the ochre-red traces are Drusilla's, but it's only an educated guess.

Coal has brought along a single cue card, the cardboard edges beginning to swell from holding it too long in her hands. She lays the sweaty card in her lap. "COMMUNITY BUILDING," it says at the top, with four bullet points:

- Valuing and encouraging our citizens without magical capabilities
- Recruiting new blood from outside the town wall
- Non-magical cottage industries
- Town expansion: from a circle to an oval

Each of her points intersects and builds off one another. If the council understands her overall vision in the next fifteen minutes, then they can follow up on the lower-level details later.

The wooden doors slide open.

In the evening, they post the rankings outside on the council's noticeboard. There's Coal's presentation alongside her name, third on the list. She's satisfied enough. Most importantly, it's two places above Porsha's.

WEDNESDAY

Wednesday is Retrieval Day. The eight remaining contestants have been loosed from the same spot outside the town wall, and are currently each speeding their way towards their chosen prey.

Being granted permission to undertake the retrieval challenge is, in itself, a high gesture of trust from the Council: few witches are granted the opportunity to mix with others outside of their community. Putting Witchville at the slightest risk is immediate grounds for disqualification, and possibly imprisonment or banishment.

There are still some ex-residents who have slipped through the system: those who abdicate from Witchville without having their memory of it removed are not forgotten. Instead, they become the targets for those participating in Retrieval Day.

Coal flies just above the treetops, careful to keep beneath the notice of any planes or balloons. The sun is only mild, but sweat has made her long-sleeve cotton shirt form a second skin against her back, and her palms are slick against her broom's handlebars for the first time this competition. She has cloaked herself in a personal version of the chameleon-like enchantment over Witchville, but it's more prone to glitching while its subject is moving. There's bile in her throat; she's miscalculated, she's made silly assumptions.

She's faster on the broom than when she was twelve, and at her current maximum speed the enchantment can't keep up properly. Her clothing is camouflage-patterned, and her hair has been doused in brown chalk, but it's still too risky to flash into visibility every few meters. She's had to consciously slow her speed by about a quarter to stay hidden, and she's gritting her teeth with the extended concentration, plus the stress of going significantly slower than she'd planned. She'll struggle to make first or second in this round. Third or fourth are also question marks. Every so often, she realises she's biting down on her tongue like a chew toy, and she shifts it towards the back of her mouth.

Closer to the city, Coal pauses every so often to animate her taxidermy sparrow and scout ahead. Finally, she removes the visual enchantment with some relief, stuffs her broom into her oversized backpack so that only the bike handles stick out, and starts sprinting between the city's beige boxes towards the apartment Suzannah Katsdaugh shares with her daughter.

Healing herself during the run means that she doesn't have to stop. She's had the route memorised for years. When Coal was thirteen and Suzannah was nineteen, Suzannah ran off with one of the rare naked men who dropped into Witchville and hadn't died on impact. The two girls had known each other by sight, and Coal had always thought Suzannah was an obvious choice. Now, Coal skids to a stop under the open window of Suzannah's modest second-floor apartment. A wooden windchime sways beneath a window box full of geraniums.

Coal allows herself a couple of deep, steadying breaths, and then guides the sparrow up again to check there's no-one to watch as she boosts herself up with her broom.

She tucks herself into the window frame like a camouflaged Peter Pan, settling her broom just inside Suzannah's small kitchen. Suzannah sits a couple of meters away, sipping tea with both hands at her lime-washed wooden dining table. She meets Coal's eyes with only the barest hint of surprise. Instead, Coal is the one unsettled, and she shifts to find better balance on the window ledge.

She recovers quickly. Coal chooses her warmest and most charming smile, and says, "Suzannah. So nice to see you again. I've come to take you home now."

Her prey takes another long sip of tea. Smells like chamomile. Suzannah says, "Honestly, there's a part of me that's tempted. But I have a life here; I have a husband, I have a son." A cluster of Texta drawings are pinned to the fridge.

"Bring them," Coal says. "Of course, we'd welcome them, too, with open arms."

"Come, now. Even if that's true, you know Witchville isn't the sort of place most outsiders can just fit into. We grew up in that single-gender society, but Steve and Cory aren't going to easily adjust to suddenly being called my wife and daughter."

Coal's fingertips dig into the window ledge. "Sure, there might be a bumpy period at the start, but you're talking as if Witchville never changes. They can learn to call your family the right things. I mean, just yesterday the council were very receptive to my presentation about bringing in new residents from outside. They know that—"

"Coal." Suzannah waits for silence. "It's not a good match. I'm not going back with you."

Coal's heart has broken into a canter. "And there's nothing I can do to change your mind?"

"Nothing." The word hangs in the air. "You've spent your entire life in Witchville. I wouldn't expect you to understand."

Coal's whole body flares with heat, like a fever. "You know what I have to do, then."

"Why?" asks Suzannah. She places down her cup, calm as always. "Steve and I haven't told anyone about Witchville, not in almost ten years. We haven't revealed anything. Haven't put anything in danger. Why would you take my memories when I've proven to be trustworthy?"

Coal tries to study Suzannah's face, which she thinks looks sincere, but Coal's vision has started to blur at the edges. Suzannah's voice sounds further away: muffled.

Coal wavers on the windowsill. Her duty to Witchville is unquestionable, but she finds herself unable to reach out and take something precious from Suzannah for no definitive reason. Within the mostly white kitchen, a vase of chrysanthemums sits on a violet napkin that looks Witchvillian. What an odd thing to take with you.

Coal gropes for her broom. She has wasted enough time here, is still wasting time, needs to find and retrieve her backup immediately.

"Fine," Coal breathes.

She barely remembers to check for observers before she drops back out the window.

WEDNESDAY EVENING

Coal breaches Witchville at 6:23 PM with Rita Safira in tow. She comes fourth out of eight, which will have to be good enough. Porsha comes third.

FRIDAY

The final challenge is a mock council meeting. Six of their town council members are democratically elected every three years, and the seventh and last seat is reserved for the most powerful witch in Witchville.

Porsha is exempt from this challenge entirely, both because the other competitors will be warming her usual chair, and because she's attended the last hundred council meetings and is very much a known entity. Coal is grateful that she won't have to see Porsha's judgemental jaw across the table.

There are six competitors left, officially, although based on their previous scores Coal knows that two of those cannot possibly win. If she aces this meeting she can still take down Porsha. She doesn't need to know everything or agree perfectly with the council; she just needs to be reasonable, and mostly articulate, and maybe inject some fresh ideas into a council that might be keen on a change. She can do this.

Coal cracks her knuckles. The doors open, and there's the polished round table she remembers from ten years ago. There's the council, with their brooches and peacock feathers and gold-plated pens. They smile and beckon her forward, and the seventh chair moulds to Coal's body like she was always meant to sit there.

FRIDAY EVENING

There is a small crowd waiting at the council noticeboard when they post the results. The official winner won't be announced until tomorrow's ceremony, but those in the know can piece together the latest rankings with the rest and predict the overall order with 99% certainty.

Coal's body buzzes like she's just channelled electricity. There are already glittering faces turned to her before she can see the list, and she's suddenly certain: she has won. She is the most powerful witch in Witchville.

There it is on the note: Coal has ranked second in the latest challenge, and Porsha is third. Her wide eyes snap to Porsha's like a magnet, and Porsha's face is stony, like someone has died.

People are congratulating her, grinning, reaching out to slap her on the back or arm or shoulder. Coal wants to bask in it, to preen, to celebrate with those bubbling cocktails that release tiny fireworks. Rion is squeezing her hand with excitement. But she finds herself backing away. "Tomorrow," she says. "Congratulate me tomorrow, when it's official."

Coal swoops towards home, pupils dilated, high on success like a hunter with her trophy, but with Porsha's dour face flashing behind her eyes. She pulls into a series of vertical loops, fumbling her way towards dizzy. The flickering lights of Witchville blur below her like burning sparklers through the air. Fuck Porsha. Coal's more than earned this. She wants to yell.

She's been home for less than five minutes when her doorbell chimes. Someone has slid a piece of thick parchment under the front door. Coal picks it up:

I wasn't going to say anything if you hadn't won. Your traces were all over Suzannah's kitchen like an anxious cat spraying. You must have been quite beside yourself to leave an ex-resident with her memories. I finished the job.

I'm sorry, truly.

The parchment shakes in Coal's thin hands. The doorbell chimes again, and of course – there are people outside waiting for her. She pushes down the dread that has erupted through her body and forces herself to meet them.

It's the council again, all six of them, and Porsha standing a little further to the back. They're not smiling this time. Coal isn't going to be announced as the most powerful witch in Witchville. Coal will probably be locked up for breaking a basic covenant.

"Come in, please," she hears herself say. "Let me just get my parents."

The council shuffles into the entry hall as Coal jogs upstairs. She struggles not to sprint. Her parents aren't at home yet; they were to return after Genevieve's theatre show to congratulate or commiserate with her. Not any more.

The sunset casts an orange-pink glow over the kitchen. Coal plucks one of Saika's wax bumblebees off the table and whispers to it: *Nicolette is down in her basement.* She flings it in the direction of the stairs, where it continues winding its way towards the council's waiting ears. That should buy her at least another thirty seconds.

She grabs one of Genevieve's wax masks and the spare broom beside the fridge. It doesn't have a seat or handlebars, but it will still fly. She smooshes the mask onto her face as her other hand cranks open a window. The wax warms and wraps itself over her face like a lover. Coal can't remember what this new face and hair looks like, but it doesn't matter, as long as it's not hers.

She was the most powerful witch in Witchville – for a good twenty minutes.

NOW

Retrieval Day is tomorrow. Coal has chosen a cottage at the farthest edge of the beige box city, but Porsha might still come for her.

She can count a thousand parts of Witchville that she misses, but she has no intention of playing the prodigal daughter, the lost girl filled with remorse. And she won't lose her memories quietly.

She reinforces the ward around the edges of her property, the one which muddles the mind and turns you around, proclaiming you have no business here. She reinforces the one two metres further in, which provides a mild forcefield. Porsha could breach that easily, but not without drawing the attention of Coal's curious neighbours. The final line of defence is a full-body hazmat suit that Coal has soaked in magical-dampening ingredients for close to a year.

No need to send up a wax sparrow. Instead, she has a taxidermy wolf to greet any unwelcome visitors with bared fangs. And a few new tricks in her arsenal, if she needs to pull out all the stops. After all, it's been an eventful five years.

And she's the most powerful witch outside Witchville.

THIS IS (NOT) MY BEAUTIFUL CAT

When the girl is six years old, she uncovers a grey and white kitten in a sagging cardboard box in her local park. She's walking there with her mother and their two large dogs, but despite this the kitten follows them out to the street, trotting three metres behind on the footpath like they're trailing a fuzzy ball of yarn.

Once the kitten reaches their front porch, the girl's mother prepares a saucer of watery milk and the girl pleads to keep him. A cushioned nest is made for him inside the house. The girl snaps photographs of him with her film camera. He is so tiny. She hopes he is hers forever.

When the woman wakes up one autumn morning, there is a cat in her house. She does not own a cat.

Her wife sits on the carpet near the open back door, patting a tense grey and white cat with wary eyes. "He just walked in," says her wife, grinning.

The woman is calm and patient, and soon she is also blessed to pat the cat a few minutes later. Its fur is so soft to stroke, like a brushtail possum. It reminds her of the fuzzy grey and white cat she had as a child.

No-one else claims the kitten, so now he belongs to the girl. He sleeps curled in the skirt of her school uniform, tucked gently in the protection of her crossed legs. She gives him a long and regal name that most adults would never consider. He grows big, and he is loved.

They're notified of the cat's visits due to its tinkling bell. When they hear the tinkles around their doors and windows, often the woman or her wife will go out to greet the cat and stroke it. They talk kindly to it. Soon the cat lets them pick it up for snuggles. Soon the cat screams at them for attention. Soon the cat is on their property all the time, and they wonder when that happened, and put out a box for the cat to curl up in because the concrete outside their back door is getting cold.

The girl and her cat are a couple of years older now, and the cat rarely comes properly inside any more. The girl doesn't know why, but perhaps it's because they have a puppy now, and the puppy likes to run and bark. Her cat still eats the name-brand cat food they scoop out for him morning and night, and he still has the enclosed back porch to rest in where it's dry and safe. Her cat is healthy, and even though she doesn't see him much any more, the girl knows that's what matters.

The woman and her wife love this cat, the cat that is not theirs. They put out bowls of water for him, which are lapped up daily, but they never feed him. They are not trying to steal a cat.

The woman worries about him outside in the cold. It gets to zero degrees Celsius sometimes. No cats are supposed to be outside in their area at all, but this cat is on their property almost all day and night. There aren't really any predators to attack him in Australia, but she worries about the main road nearby, and she worries about the weather. Why won't his owners bring him inside? He always seems generously fed and well, but she worries.

The cat burrows closer into her shoulder, purring, and the woman wishes he was hers forever.

The girl is almost a teenager, and her cat is stretched long in the sunshine near their back door, which doesn't happen very often these days. She kneels next to him and strokes him reverently. His fur is so warm, his eyes so green. She knows he will die someday, like all humans and animals do, so she is saving this moment in her mind. She tries to pour all of her love into her hands and capture him perfectly in her memory, so sweet and vital.

The woman buys a $35 microchip scanner from eBay and scans the cat that is not hers. She plus the microchip number into an internet database. Because she is not a vet or other authorised body it won't give her the cat's name or address, but it does say that the cat was born twenty-seven years ago and is deceased. The woman tosses the microchip scanner in the bin; she supposes you get what you pay for.

Then she snuggles the cat and says, "Is it time for dinner?" The cat butts his cheek against her own, eyes closed with affection, and then jumps down to find his evening meal. He climbs over the woman's fence, runs through two yards, and then darts under a gate... Where he crosses through space and time and arrives in the girl's garden for dinner.

LOVELY LILAS

The reason Trent from Pionnarm contacts me: in a survey of 300 people, several respondents said I was the loveliest person they knew.

Pionnarm wants to copy my personality. They want to sell it as one of the software options for their new android model: Lovely Lila. Customers can also choose from Sultry Samantha, Playful Peyton, Whimsical Willow, or Cool Cherry, which makes me think of a car paint colour more than a woman's name.

Copying my personality would only take a few hours, Trent says, and wouldn't hurt at all. They'd offer generous compensation.

"And what about the copies of me?" I ask. Would they hurt? Would they feel things if their owners were cruel to them, or neglectful, or decided that the vibe of the month called for Sultry Samantha and asked for an overwrite?

"They won't feel anything," Trent assures me. So I agree.

Pionnarm calls to see if I want a complimentary Lovely Lila shipped out to me. Basic physical customisation of my choice. The idea of any android staring at me inside of my otherwise empty apartment is off-putting. "Thank you, but I don't think I'm your target audience," I say, and quickly decline.

I start to notice them on the streets before Pionnarm says they're officially on sale: the Lilas. Their appearances vary, customised by their owners, so I can never be definitively sure. But I recognise the software: the smile they make when they're moderating themselves, and the smile they make when they're not. The reassuring looks they give their owners. The way they fold their hands politely, like they're holding hands with themselves. The same expression they wear whenever they point out a nice sculpture, or a dog, or compliment their owner's pinstripe shirt.

They really are lovely.

#

I pick a daisy for a Lila by the water fountain, and press it into her hand before her owner sees. I write a poem for the Lila cross-legged at a train station. I start carrying wrapped bonbons and a rainbow of origami cranes in my bag.

Trent promised me that the Lilas can't feel anything, but I like seeing their expressions of pleasant surprise when I give them these gifts, however superficial.

Finally, I call Pionnarm: would they still send me a complimentary copy?

There is a Lila in my apartment now. I lie on the couch with my head on her lap, while she strokes my hair. I feel warm, and full. Later, we will make each other hot chocolates and do some reading, and then one of us will point out the moon.

She is more than enough; she is plenty.

So I must be, too.

THE ORCHARD

I've been allocated the front seat because my twenty-eight-year-old legs
fit better there – the rest of my competition, children between the ages of
nine and fourteen, are comfortable in the back of the mini-van. They've
spent the twenty-minute ride discussing school, Snapchat, Minecraft and

a couple of other games or apps I haven't heard of and don't understand. I took a week off work for this, caught a train for almost three hours, spent a few hundred dollars in preparation. Now, instead, I have a persistent stomach ache and my considerable regret.

What on earth is the appeal, for children, of taking over a fruit orchard?

Finally the van pulls up at a wrought iron gate: it seems enormous for a private property, almost twice my height. A thick crimson ribbon has been tied to each outer gate post and around the tight line of trees on each side of the gate. If it's supposed to welcome the kids, it's certainly a strange way of doing so; the ribbons are visibly faded and continue so far along the tree line that I can't see their other ends.

"This is where I leave you," announces Carina. She adjusts the ochre-coloured bandana tied underneath her braid. "Sorry I can't help you take the bags up."

"Wait," says Brandon, the older, freckled boy. "You're not coming with us?"

"Nope." Carina shuts the empty boot. "I'm not allowed past the gate. I've never seen any further than this." She winks at the kids, but nonetheless I don't think she's joking. "You guys are lucky."

A couple of jaws drop. Whilst we pick up our dusty luggage, Carina unlocks the gate with a large silver key. The four kids and I pass through; it's secured again behind us.

The van reverses away.

We crest a hill and the farmhouse appears. I can't decide whether to be impressed or not – it's unusually wide for a house, with a smaller second storey and a large chimney sticking out of the centre of it all, like a blocky pyramid. The whole building looks bitsy, like the construction equivalent of a patchwork quilt, and all the parts seem well-made but needing some care. Smoke spirals cheerfully from the chimney.

"Whoa, check it out," says Brandon. The youngest kid, Jemima, is already running the last two hundred metres to the front door.

As the rest of us keep walking, a woman steps out onto the front porch: brown slip dress and crimson gloves. Jemima launches herself into the woman's arms. The woman catches her. I wonder if they know each other.

When the rest of us reach the porch Jemima has settled back on the floor, and the woman reaches out to shake my hand. Her gloves are soft leather against my fingers. Her shoes are walking boots, and her simple dress laces up in the back like a loose corset. "I'm Bridgette," she says, "and this is my land. Welcome, all of you."

My other hand tightens around my suitcase handle. She's beautiful.

"Come in, come in," she says. "I'll show you to your rooms. Then we'll have some lunch."

Inside, Bridgette's décor is an eclectic mix of muted patterns, hanging plants, and expensive highlights. None of her sofas match. Flowering vines crawl over hardwood and shining geometric light fittings. Damn, *damn*, I kind of love it here.

Past the living room and off a long corridor with botanical wallpaper, the kids and I have one small bedroom each. Mine is the last one. We're supposed to have twenty minutes to settle in between now and lunch, but I catch Bridgette with a touch to her shoulder.

"Listen," I say quietly, "there's obviously been some mistake. This was a competition for children, and it's ridiculous for me to even be here. I completely understand if you want me to go."

She's looking at me with a very tolerant smile – it makes me feel about as old as the kids. "There was no age limit on the competition, Emily. Mostly children were good at it, so mostly children got in." Her lips twitch towards a smirk. "Really, you should stay. You're the one at a disadvantage here. If you happen to win, you'll very much deserve it."

I am left to simmer in my embarrassment.

Lunch is essentially a friendly interview interspersed with food. I was expecting staff at the competition – administrators, cooks, gardeners – but we haven't seen anyone since Carina. Bridgette serves up a steaming vegetable soup with a slight chilli kick. There are Christmas crackers on the table even though it's April; we pop them, we wear the paper crowns. We drink peach iced tea with plastic curly straws. Finally, we lock our five mobile phones in Bridgette's miniature safe, and it's time for a proper introduction to the competition.

Bridgette has the five of us line up beside the back door. One by one, she secures cotton blindfolds firmly over our eyes, so that I can't see anything beyond a sliver of my own feet. I hear the quiet swish of the back door sliding open, and then her gloved hand is secure in mine. I grasp Sierra's hand on the other side of me, and then we're pulled gently outside, all of us trailing over the grass after Bridgette like a human daisy chain.

"Now, when we arrive," Bridgette announces, "you must all promise me not to move towards anything. Not to touch anything. If you do, you will be immediately disqualified from the competition. Do you understand?"

Several variations of 'Yes' and 'Uh-huh' travel up from further down the line, and I quickly offer up my own. My brain is busy projecting half-a-dozen possibilities onto the backs of my eyelids, about what exactly we might not be allowed to touch. I expect the children to start whispering again to one another, but now they're silent as snowfall.

Bridgette slows and then halts quicker than I am expecting, and I only barely prevent myself from running into her. The grounding warmth of her hand sweeps away. "Okay," she says after a moment. "You can take off your blindfolds."

At first I think I'm looking at a painting. It takes my brain a few seconds to register the lack of canvas edges, the absence of brush strokes and understand that yes, all signs seem to point to this being real life.

The six of us stand in front of several rows of trees; trees unlike any I've seen or even imagined. Each one of them is large, at least four times my height and with trunks about six feet in diameter, but every one of them is a work of art:

A tree with waxy honeycombs instead of bark, with a viscous waterfall of honey spiralling down from its canopy and down into the earth. Bees the size of my feet dart between levitating cherry blossom flowers, leaving behind trails of sparkling smoke in their wake.

A tree of gold and silver latticework, a rainbow of gems embedded throughout in a hundred different sizes. The smaller branches are hinged, and one opens to reveal a violet-coloured animal, somewhere between a red panda and a fox, with giant, six-sided gemstone eyes. It scuttles along, pries off a gem with its raptor-like claws, and disappears with its prize into the hole it came from.

A bone tree with a spiral of steps carved into the trunk. Strings of thousands of teeth drip down around it like a veil, like the leaves of a willow tree. Some of the teeth shine with chips or coatings of metal, like they had holes fixed with dental fillings.

And the trees keep stretching back and back, made of candy or muscle or patchwork cotton or surrounded with floating halos of water. My mind is reeling. One of the kids starts to swear and then pauses mid-word.

"I have filled about one-third of this land already," says Bridgette, and I tear my eyes away to meet her gaze. "And I plan to fill another third. The last third will be filled by the winner of this competition, who will become my assistant and take care of this place in my absence, and who will inherit it after I die." She smiles at our gaping faces. I think I spot a twinkle in her caramel eyes. "Welcome to the orchard."

\#

We wander back to the house, and it's like an extra layer of colour and magic has infused everything we pass. Tiny daisies and violets dot the lush grass beneath our shoes. Bridgette has a sizable garden planted past the house's back door, loosely surrounded by a porcelain picket fence, which we missed the first time because of our blindfolds. I spy a clump of huge fanged flycatchers, snapdragons the colours of sunsets, cerulean caterpillars the size of my thumb, and beetles so shiny they look like mirrors. Tiny white hummingbirds swarm over red rose vines. Neon koi glow inside their semi-circular pond.

We pass through the sliding door again, and Bridgette puts the kettle on. She likes to answer questions with a warm cup in her hands, cross-legged on the most central couch.

Question: How do you win?

Answer: By being the last one left.

Question: How do you do that?

Answer: You make the best trees. You plant a small object in the ground, cover it with soil, and then run back so you don't get hurt by the tree coming up. It happens very quickly.

Bridgette peels off her gloves to show us her visibly altered hands – shiny, paler bolts of scar tissue cross her palms; she wasn't quick enough, the first couple of times – and then redresses them in leather.

Question: How do you know what makes the best trees?

Answer: You make an educated guess, based on what might come out. Don't just pick something because it looks cool; I want interesting, original, and personal choices. I asked you to bring a few important sentimental items with you for a reason. But please don't use anything you can't bear to part with, because you won't get it back.

Question: How long do we have?

Answer: The first round will be late tomorrow morning. Then we'll have lunch, and then Carina will arrive, and one of you will be leaving with her. So don't save your best seed until later – every time we plant anything, it really counts.

At this point there's a quiet bang, and a black, furry creature appears in Bridgette's living room via a medium-sized doggie door. As it gets closer, I can see it resembles an oversized cat, if cats had pouches on their bellies and six prehensile tails. It flicks its clover-green eyes across the group of us, makes a squeaky sound like an inconvenienced fox, and uncurls one of its tails to drop a bird of paradise flower into Bridgette's lap.

Bridgette claps once with obvious delight, rocking back a little on the couch, and then runs her gloved fingers down its head and back. "Everyone," she says, "this is Marigold. She's very intelligent. I asked her, and a few others, to stay away until you'd see the trees, but they should be coming back now." She scratches the side of Marigold's neck, eyes crinkling in affection. "Say hello, Marigold."

The cat eyes us again, and then arranges its tails in a very clear 'Hi' formation. The children gasp and squeal, and Jemima waves rapidly in response.

Bridgette lifts Marigold up on the couch with her. "You know most of the rules already, but the last ones are: you may be allowed to use something from this house or the gardens as a seed, but you must ask permission before taking it. And you're welcome to walk around the orchard, but don't go too near the trees, and if you're under eighteen then I expect you to do so in pairs."

She smiles slowly – a deeply satisfied smile – and then waves her hand to dismiss us. The children break into pairs and race back out towards the orchard. They're beaming and yelping and tapping each other like this is their first visit to Disneyland. They asked all the questions, and I asked none, paralysed on one of Bridgette's embroidered lounge chairs. Maybe this is part of what she meant by my disadvantage.

Bridgette's cup clinks down on the glass coffee table. I meet her eyes, expecting judgment, but they're gentle. "Emily," she says. "Goodness knows I don't get a lot of human visitors. But may I recommend a nap, and then some more iced tea, and then a stroll around the orchard? After a big change sometimes the brain just needs to re-set itself." She strokes a finger down between Marigold's eyes. "Turn it off and on again, so to speak. You'll have enough time."

The nap really does help. When I wake things feel clearer, more solid. I feel a little more like I'm meant to be here.

Bridgette is in the kitchen when I emerge, and there's talking and the watery clank of washing dishes, but the rest of the room looks empty and she's leaning on a counter away from the sink. Then she moves slightly and I see flashes of movement and shine, like dragonfly wings. She motions me closer.

Tiny women the size of Barbie dolls are scrubbing, dunking and drying our lunchtime dishes. Opalescent, insect-like wings protrude from their backs. "Fairies?" I whisper.

"That's not what they call themselves," says Bridgette, "But it's close enough. They are my very dear companions who also look after the house and grounds. They also built the rooms you're staying in, and are excellent conversationalists. Just don't expect them to be able to fly very far. They can get perhaps two feet off the ground. They're better at climbing."

One of the fairies dives under the dishwater for a moment to pull the plug, and then squeezes out her cobalt hair while another wrings the dishcloth and springs up to hang the cloth over the tap, wings buzzing like a hummingbird. Bridgette pours me an iced tea, as promised.

The cobalt fairy holds out her doll-sized hand for me to take. "So pleased to meet you," she says, with a sharp accent I can't place and with a lower voice than I was expecting. "We're totally starved of new company."

I spend the next twenty minutes conversing with Bridgette and the fairies – or attempting to, because comprehension is sometimes a challenge for me when there are *mythical creatures* two feet away. I do learn that there are twelve of them in all, not just three, and that they've been here about four years, ever since Bridgette planted a lemongrass soap tree and part of what emerged was fairy-printed fabric. Now that fabric sits across Bridgette's kitchen window as lemon-butter-coloured curtains, and the fairies come and go as they please, merging into and out of their printed silhouettes.

Then I make a slow lap of the trees in the orchard, and my mind processes them better this time. The kids are still running around like it's a playground, but at least they're keeping a reasonable berth from the trees themselves. I examine each trunk, canopy and root system as I pass, hoping for inspiration to strike. I wander between trees that look like living subway maps, trees with keys of every colour and shape knotted into their shoots, trees that just look like a column of pigeons stacked on top of one another, blinking and puffed up for the winter.

Back in my room I lay out the contents of my suitcase across the cornflower blue carpet, and think, *what on earth is here that I can use?* I pass my eyes and hands over my more sentimental items a dozen times: a framed photo of my parents; a plastic cake knife – a prop from my favourite musical; a faded dog collar; a plastic ice-skating medal; an old wedding ring. None of them seem like they would make even half-decent trees.

Just as my brain threatens to shut down again, Timmy knocks nervously on my door and says, "Sierra's drawing trees on everyone in Sharpie. Do you want one, too?"

I think of how bad that would be for my skin, plus the awful Sharpie fumes. "Sure, I do."

#

We've rolled dice to determine the order we plant in; this time it's Timmy, Brandon, Jemima, me and finally Sierra.

Bridgette's marked the exact spots where we're supposed to dig; Timmy finds the grass that's been coloured with Sierra's red Sharpie. He crouches and opens his fist to reveal a sweaty USB stick, then buries it the way Bridgette has taught us: by digging a small hole in the dirt with both hands, placing his seed, and smoothing the soil back over the top.

As soon as the USB is covered he bolts away. The ground has already started to vibrate under our feet, and there's an audible rumble for a moment before a great black tree erupts where Timmy was crouched seconds ago. It spirals out of the ground like a corkscrew, and as its growth slows I can read the numbers that make up the trunk: a dense stream of ones and zeros. A very real crocodile runs up and down the spiral, jaw open to showcase its teeth.

"Don't worry," says Bridgette, sounding only mildly concerned, "it shouldn't leave the tree unless provoked."

Back at home, Timmy had coded the first part of a smartphone game about a crocodile paddling through space.

We move on.

Brandon plants a cluster of interlocking colourful plastic, which I recognise as broken off from one of his Nerf guns. The tree that sprouts is an intricate pillar of plastic, as if someone's designed a huge tree-house out of magical Lego. Its neon orange shutters wave gently in the wind.

Jemima plants a small metal container with a screw top; perhaps it used to have lip gloss inside. I can't tell what she's filled it with now, but when the earth parts the tree that grows is made of water. Water in the shape of a fir tree, with fabric cartoon monsters floating inside. The monsters circle each other, gnashing their teeth and swiping their claws.

Then it's my turn, and I find my hands shaking as I plant my sorry excuse for a seed. I've wrapped the ribbon from my suitcase around the prop knife from my favourite musical, Twelve Birthdays. I stumble as I retreat. The tree that sprouts is a stunted mess of ribbon and melted pink plastic, barely as tall as I am, and I feel my whole body sink with embarrassment and disappointment.

But there's a small hole at the top of the tree, and slowly, slowly, white fairy-floss-like clouds begin to billow out. They puff and snowball until they've surrounded the tip of the tree like a dandelion head. And then music begins to seep from the hole instead, sweet and simple in the country air.

My fingernails gradually detract from where they've been digging into the heel of my palm.

Sierra is last. She's chosen her late father's cigarette lighter. The tree that emerges is made of patterned metal filigree, with flames burning inside like a giant metal lantern. Through the holes in the metal we can see the fire flickering, changing colours to turn into fleeting images: an Indian man holding his daughters, sipping his coffee, adjusting his tie.

I glance at Sierra. "He gave up about ten years ago," she says, and I notice the tears on her cheeks. "But he carried it with him every day, anyway, in case it was needed. And then I did."

We watch for several minutes. We watch until Bridgette puts her hand on Sierra's shoulder, and we head inside for lunch.

Lunch, as prepared by the fairies, is roast lamb with mint jelly and cranberry sauce, and it's just about the best roast I've ever tasted. I expected the atmosphere to be awkward around the table, but the kids chat as though one of us isn't going home today: exclamations of *so-and-so's tree was SO cool* and endless questions about the fairies and magic to Bridgette, some of which she can answer and many she can't.

Perhaps they're all foolishly sure, like me, that someone else's tree was worse and so they must be safe.

Bridgette asks us all to stand once we've finished eating. She walks off into the kitchen without explanation, and the kids' cheery conversation rolls to a halt. Sierra grips the back of her chair. Timmy runs his hand across the back of his neck. Jemima smooths her hands down her skirt, and Brandon rocks slightly from side to side.

Bridgette returns with a tray of five porcelain tea cups. Gold on the outside, white on the inside, and full of a steaming, opaque red liquid. She places each cup very deliberately in front of each of us, and then steps away from the table.

"At the bottom of each of these cups is a symbol. If you have a red circle underneath your tea, that means I am inviting you to stay another day. If you have a red cross there instead, you will be driving back with Carina this afternoon."

"Noughts and crosses," Sierra murmurs, and Bridgette smiles briefly.

The next five minutes or so stretches on like taffy. We stand in relative silence as our cups cool, taking tiny sips of sweet, cinnamon-flavoured tea, burning our lips and tongues, both eager and dreading the picture on the bottom.

Finally, my tea has reached a more acceptable temperature. I gulp down the remaining half with my eyes squeezed shut, and then pop them open one at a time. Clearly visible through the last remnants of liquid and a smattering of tea leaves, there it is: a perfect, beautiful circle in foxtail red.

I look up: Sierra is smiling, her empty cup resting on the table. Jemima grins silently, cradling her cup to her chest. The boys are still finishing their tea. Brandon finally pulls his cup back with knitted brows, and then almost drops it on the tiled floor.

"What?" he says, and then makes an effort to lower his voice. "It's me?"

Bridgette puts a gentle hand on his shoulder. "I'm sorry, Brandon; someone had to go. Grab your bag, please, and I'll take you down to the gate."

We wave Brandon off from the front porch. The remainder of the afternoon involves the children enjoying supervised chats with their parents from Bridgette's landline, some impromptu games of Four Square and Dungeons-and-Dragons-themed Cluedo, and me wandering throughout the house and orchard for additional tree ideas.

As we're packing away the board game pieces I ask the children why they applied for this competition when they still thought it was for a regular, non-magical orchard. With slightly hunched shoulders, Timmy says that his parents thought the land, and possibly the orchard itself, would be worth a lot of money.

Sierra nods in agreement. "And that 'Agrarian Ambassador' would look good on university applications."

"There might've been horses!" Jemima adds, and that her parents almost didn't let her come. They're now staying in a hotel nearby in case she needs them.

After dinner, Bridgette invites me to have a wine with her, if I haven't already planned to use that time for something else. I haven't.

So we tuck ourselves into either end of the turquoise velvet couch. She swirls the red wine gently in her cup. "I really liked your application."

Oh God. I hurry to swallow my mouthful. I'd always pictured the competition judges as a bespectacled panel of baby boomers, and had stupidly not amended that picture after arriving here. Bridgette must be able to see me burning up.

"Oh," I manage. "I – You read it. Thank you."

"Tell me: you already have your own adult life back at home. Why would you want to drop everything to come here?"

I press myself back into the corner of the couch. "I don't really, though. I mean, I don't have a life," I amend. "I thought I would have one. What I do have now is a job that's going nowhere and no partner and no family. So not a lot to drop, really."

When I can bear to glance up, Bridgette's looking me right in the eyes and smiling softly, and somehow it only makes me feel a smidgen more embarrassed. "Well," she says, "I'm sorry things didn't work out as you planned. Life can be terribly unkind."

"It can." I pick up my wineglass again, even though I'm not keen on red wine, because it's comforting to hold. "I'm hoping new things will be better."

I watch her take another sip of wine. Study the delicate laugh lines around her eyes. The quirk of her mouth. The way her gloved hand cradles her glass.

"I'm glad you're here, Emily," she says.

Breath by breath, I feel my coiled muscles start to unwind. "I'm glad I'm here, too."

Bridgette retires to her bedroom soon after, and I stay on the couch smoothing the velvet under my bare feet. There's a faint imprint in the fibres from where Bridgette was sitting. If I look over my shoulder, I can see the waxing gibbous moon outside the glass door. And then someone stage-whispers my name.

The cobalt-haired fairy half-flies, half-climbs up the couch leg and waves her tiny hand. She removes a detached fairy wing from where it's been tucked down the front of her tulle dress and scoots over to present it to me. "You can use this tomorrow."

My hand twitches towards it. "Isn't that cheating?"

"Why would it be? You're allowed to use something that's already here, with its owner's permission, and it's given freely."

I check to see if any of her wings are missing, but they all appear intact. Do fairies shed? I pinch the wing gently between my fingers, thin and fragile like cellophane. "Are you helping all of us?"

Her mouth contorts like she's trying not to laugh. "Hardly. We want you to stay. Bridgette likes you, we can tell." She winks, exaggerated so I can't miss it in the dim light.

"Likes me?"

"No harm in a little matchmaking." She pads over to the edge of the couch. "Use it," she demands, and flutters to the floor.

Because I can come up with no better plan and am slowly acknowledging that I *do* want to win, I do plant the wing the following morning, having wrapped it carefully in my favourite sterling silver chain.

The tree that emerges resembles a futuristic office building, layers of metal floors divided by shiny, translucent walls clearly modelled after fairy wings. Tiny blue veins map the whole structure, and between every few floors pulses a white, fleshy sphere that immediately reminds me of a heart. Fairies much smaller than I'm used to swarm and disperse throughout the tree like harried bees.

We plant in the opposite order to yesterday, with Sierra first. She plants three tubes of her oil paints tied together with an elastic band, and the tree that emerges looks entirely made of paint, like it was plucked from a canvas and transformed into enormous 3D. You can see each individual brush stroke that composes it from roots to tip.

Jemima plants a masquerade mask, the kind that would cover the whole top half of her face if she wore the elastic. It looks like she's coloured it herself with primary school markers and paints. Its tree is a mass of tightly packed dirt with hundreds of masks dangling from the branches like overripe fruit. Masks of dozens of materials and in every possible shape. And from a couple of higher branches, I see what looks like a few masks made from human skin.

I don't quite see what Timmy's seeds are. They look like a miscellaneous mess cupped deep in his child hands. I ask him later and he says: two eyes from an action figure and three twigs covered in chin blood. When his tree sprouts it seems to be an ordinary oak tree, the most ordinary tree in the orchard, but then its branches shiver and three slits open in its trunk: two large eyes that could have been transplanted from a giant doll, and a smiling gash of a wooden mouth trickling with sap and blood.

"Nice to meet you," growls Timmy's tree.

We sip the cinnamon tea from the porcelain teacups. My heart beats against my chest like a battering ram, and I have to sit down to finish so I don't spill anything.

I latch my eyes closed again to empty the cup. Before I can force myself to open them, Sierra says, "Oh!" like she's stepped on a Lego.

Over my own red circle I spot her struggling to compose herself. "I, um, wasn't expecting that," she says. Pinpricks of tears are welling in the corners of her eyes. "You guys all did really good. Keep it up. Good luck with the rest of everything."

Bridgette takes Sierra's cup with care. "Your tree was really lovely, Sierra. I'm so glad it's a part of the orchard."

Sierra's face reads *Not lovely enough*, but only for a moment. Then she's hugging Bridgette and the rest of us with what seems to be genuine affection, and going to collect her bag with dry eyes.

After dinner, Bridgette and I tuck ourselves back into the ends of the turquoise couch. I've declined another glass of wine, but Bridgette has one, and has a fire crackling in the nearby fireplace. Our sock-covered toes touch in the middle of the couch. My feet are basking, euphoric, in the warmth of the flames and her body heat. Neither of us has moved them away.

"Aren't you worried they'll tell someone?" I say. "Brandon and Sierra, when they get back?"

"Oh no." Bridgette winks at me above her glass. "I have my tea."

It takes me a couple of seconds, but I say, "The red tea? With the noughts and crosses?"

She nods around a mouthful of wine. "If you have a cross, then your tea is a little different. By the time you reach the gate you'll have forgotten anything magic, anything fantastic about this place. It's just a regular orchard."

This knowledge drops inside me like a shotput. The loss. My hands come up to wrap around my neck like armour.

"I need my precautions," Bridgette continues. "Like the ribbon around the grounds. It's a ward so that no-one can see what this place really looks like, from the ground or from the air."

"Of course," I say, but the fire is much too hot now, like I'm going to burn right through the bottom of the couch. The living room is blurring, so I stare at my legs.

Bridgette's gloved hands come to rest on my shins. "Emily?"

"I'll forget all of this," I say, and am surprised at the emotion thick in my voice. "And it's..." *The most amazing thing to ever happen to me.* I take a pint-sized gasp of air. "Because I'm going to lose."

"Oh, Emily," she says, and again I'm surprised by the lack of judgement. "If I didn't think you could win I wouldn't have invited you." She holds out her gloves, the firelight playing gently over the crimson leather. "Take off my gloves."

I scoot forward and pull the leather off her fingers one by one, a centimetre at a time, and hear my breath slow as I work. By the time I'm working my fingers under the cuffs, brushing my fingertips against her palms, my breathing is almost normal.

Bridgette places the gloves on the coffee table. She leans forward and cups my cheeks with her hands. Her fingers are warm from the gloves and the fire, but the scars across her palms are still chilled. I shiver.

"Is this okay?" she asks.

"Yes," I say.

She uncurls her legs, and then picks mine up so they're stretched over her lap.

"Is this okay?"

"Yes," I say.

She's closer and closer, and then she's kissing me. Her lips are softer than the turquoise velvet, softer than snakeskin. She smells of woodsmoke and cherries and mint. Her hand wraps around the back of my neck, warm outer and cold middle. The shotput has dislodged from my belly, and in its place my torso is filling with helium, my arms and legs are blooming with cherry blossoms.

I entwine my fingers with her free hand and break the kiss to breathe. "I, uh, don't want to win because of this."

She chuckles low in her throat. "Don't worry, you definitely won't." And Bridgette kisses me again.

She leaves me alone about ten minutes later, with swollen lips and half a glass of wine she's forgotten to finish. I carry it to the sink and let my fingertips flutter over the places she's touched me: cheeks, chin, lips, neck, waist, her legs under the back of my thighs.

I make myself a glass of water. Once I'm feeling a little less heady, I turn my attention to finding a seed for tomorrow. I'm going to win, and I'm going to do it myself, without any more help. It's only ten to ten at night. There's still time.

I head back to my room and pick through every last one of my possessions, turning out the pockets for trinkets I could have missed, emptying my handbag on my bed, tossing out the contents of my suitcase. I amass a small collection of lint-covered coins, hair ties and USB drives loaded with years-old documents. I find a couple of receipts, to-do lists and the start of a poem. Finally, running my hands around the inside walls of my suitcase, I feel something more promising.

I unzip the large pocket in the roof of my suitcase, the one I barely use as it's too thin to put more than a couple of t-shirts in, and pull out a small wad of papers. My divorce papers, lodged in amongst some other identification documents. This particular copy looks very well-loved, all rubbed around the edges and with smudged ink where my tears sank into the paper. There's a grease stain from ramen noodles on pages 2-4. The bottom corners are all warped from the sweat of my right hand. The second-last page has a tiny streak of blood from a paper cut.

I roll up the divorce papers like a runner's baton. A pleasant, low buzz of adrenaline courses through me.

This – this could be something amazing.

Jemima plants first. Her seeds look like an ordinary handful of dried leaves, but her tree sprouts up in four stages: the trunk surrounded by blossoming tulips and wildflowers, the lower branches full and thick with spearmint-green leaves, the middle autumnal with crisp leaves drifting from their moorings, the top bare except for a heavy coat of snow. She giggles and bites her fingertips.

Timmy buries a small gift box, shiny white with a candy-pink ribbon. His tree emerges fully covered in charcoal fur. A dozen bottle-green eyes blink at us from where they're sprinkled through its pelt, and tiny replicas of the gift box are tied with ribbons to the ends of several furry twigs. The wind blows one of them loose and Timmy hurries to collect it, but these new boxes are empty.

I kiss my rolled-up divorce papers before tucking them into their hole, feeling foolish and hopeful but mostly numb, which is usual for when I want something bad enough but may not get it. The tree shoots up like a swimmer desperate for air, short and thick with only a smattering of naked branches at the canopy, like a stout and leafless palm tree. Its trunk is covered in scabs where others would have bark, solid and layered and peeling. As we watch, some of the scabs fall away, leaving flickering pictures in the blood: people kneeling, weeping; slamming doors and suitcases; angry silhouettes curling into themselves – but also the joyful kneeling of proposals, comfortable embraces, kisses and gift-giving. Before long, the images fade and the blood drips down, leaving only patches of perfect white paper in their place.

Lunch is the most subdued meal we've had. Jemima explains the origin of her seeds: that she collected the leaves (and one twig) of a tree in her yard throughout the year and kept them in a Pokémon tin. Timmy is sullen: he keeps sneaking glances into his empty gift box like he's prodding at a loose tooth. When prompted, he says he was expecting some kind of cat bonanza, like if Christmas came early and Santa brought everyone kittens. Marigold weaves around my legs, and when I reach down I notice a clump of her fur has been snipped off. Bridgette folds origami animals for everyone out of napkins to try to raise the mood. She winks as she hands me my paper rabbit, and takes a brief moment to squeeze my outstretched fingers. I half expect it to come to life.

We take our cinnamon tea like it's medicine. No-one seems to be rushing this time. I still finish first, eyes wide open this time, like if I keep watching it can't hurt me. And it's a big satisfying red nought that fills me all the way up.

When the others stop sipping they're completely silent. Jemima and Timmy look straight at each other, and put down their cups at the same time, identical wide-eyed pain on their faces. I'm hit with the unexpected thought that the competition might be over already – that they might both be going home.

But Jemima breaks their eye contact. "I'm sorry, Timmy," she says.

And Timmy musters a sad little smile. He nods at everyone and leaves without another word.

After Jemima has been tucked into bed, Bridgette and I head behind the house to moon-watch. Underneath the filter of darkness, the back garden still shimmers where moonlight glances off beetles and koi, or where fireflies swirl between pockets of fern fronds. We settle on a pair of wrought iron chairs, and Bridgette explains how she inherited the orchard from her grandmother, who knew of its magical potential but had chosen to opt-out. When Bridgette moved in, there had been a single otherworldly tree hidden within wooden stakes, connected by a square of black ribbon.

When she's finished her story, Bridgette unhinges a rectangular metal tin decorated with Van Gogh's 'The Starry Night.' There are several white lumps inside, all glossy with icing. "Take a bite," she offers, "But promise you won't let go of my arm."

She probably can't see my quirked eyebrow in the darkness. I take a solid grip on her lower arm and sink my teeth into one of the desserts. It tastes like marzipan, like coffee cream, like popping candy. The popping sensation spreads down my body like a wave; a bubbling, a fizzing, a lightness. I drop the half-eaten iced lump onto the iron table. I can no longer feel the metal of the chair against my legs. I am rising. I am floating in the air like a helium balloon, anchored to Bridgette like her arm has my string.

Bridgette laughs with joy and swallows a mouthful of her own dessert. She rises to meet me like it's effortless and we float higher and higher, until we're just above the garden, until we're level with the first-storey roof. I gaze at Bridgette, wide-eyed, but she only looks blissful.

"This is what I wanted to show you!" she calls, louder than necessary given we're clutching each other's forearms. "Do you like it? It's perfectly safe, I promise; we won't get much higher, and we'll drop down again after about twenty minutes. But isn't it fun?"

I am overcome. A light wind is pushing us slowly away from the house, so I can see all of the back garden from the air and much of the orchard stretching out before us. Bridgette is smiling at me, so wide and so affectionate. I feel the freedom of weightlessness, like being suspended in the middle of a swimming pool. And in a sudden, uncontrollable rush I start to weep, and can hear it as a thick waver in my voice.

"I love it," I say. "It's the best thing ever. But I don't want to lose it tomorrow."

Bridgette isn't smiling anymore. "You keep talking about what you don't want," she says. "Stop. Tell me what you *do* want."

"I..." I squeeze the flesh of her arm until it hurts my hand. I feel like I'm about to be sucked into space. "I want to win the competition. I want to look after the orchard. Plant things in it. I want to stay. I want to stay here with you. I want to *be*... with you."

I force myself to look at her. It's hard to read Bridgette's expression in the dark, but she's nodding. "Thank you," she says gently. "That means so much to me."

I wipe at my eyes with my free hand.

"Please try to enjoy yourself."

And I take a couple of minutes to recover, but we're *flying*, and it's beautiful, and then I laugh and don't know why.

I plant our two half-eaten desserts. I expect their tree to be somehow symbolic of our affection, of hope, some kind of mixture of our saliva – something charming and romantic. What sprouts is a gorgeous, leafless giant, trunk and branches all made of hardened icing with a hill of powdered sugar around the base. It's lovely in its simplicity, but it's far too simple. Even when the tree disconnects from the soil and levitates above the powdered sugar hill, roots swaying in the breeze, I know it won't be enough to win.

Jemima has come to the final planting empty-handed. When Bridgette asks her about it, she says she has her seed inside her shoes. And she wants my help with getting it out. I am a little stunned, but have no reason to refuse. I follow her to the patch of grass which will be the competition's last planting site.

Instead of crouching like we usually do, Jemima sits firmly on the grass. She takes off one buckled leather shoe, and one frilly white sock, and I peer inside them for secrets but they appear to be empty. I don't understand how I'm expected to help. And then Jemima removes the whole lower half of her left leg, and holds its skin-coloured plastic straight up to make sure I've seen. Underneath her skirt, her flesh-and-blood leg finishes just above the knee.

As she scoops out a hole large enough for her prosthetic leg, I ask, "Are you sure you want to use that?"

"I'm sure," she says. "I have a spare in my bag back at the house. I just need you to pull me to safety, please."

I nod vacantly. I have been beaten fairly by a child a third my age. When she finishes planting I grab her swiftly under the arms, scooping her away from her winning tree, with neither of us acquiring so much as a scratch.

Bridgette escorts me down towards the bottom of the hill. I have dutifully drunk the awful tea. I try to tie the memories of magic around my mind like strings around my fingers, but I know they will come undone. I have written several notes to myself with Sierra's old Sharpie, scrawled across my stomach underneath my breasts. They will probably read like words penned while half-asleep in the earliest hours of the morning. I will not understand. Magic evaporates in the daytime. Magic loses its power against the bleakness of the everyday.

But I do not want to steep in such a black mood for Bridgette's final goodbye. I try to shrug off some of my heaviness and concentrate on her hand in mine. That, I should still remember. She's taken off one of her gloves, where she's holding me, and her skin is both soft and corded, warm and chilling from her scarring. The unworn glove pokes out of her breast pocket like a corsage.

I study the vibrancy of the grass, peppered with tiny daisies, and the solidity of the trees flanking the wrought iron gate. The sun bathes us in perfect light, and within moments my dark mood seems to fall away like an old skin. Why on earth should I mourn the loss of a fruit orchard that I never really wanted? If anything, surely the loss is–

"Listen," I say, pausing about twenty paces to the gate. "I can barely keep a cactus alive. I don't know why I thought I would be any good with an orchard. But I have so enjoyed meeting you. Perhaps, even though I didn't win, you might like to join me for dinner sometime? I could maybe come back down here in a couple of weeks?"

I've never seen Bridgette caught off-guard before, and feel immediately anxious that I've said something wrong, that she's going to take her hand away...

"You don't want the orchard anymore," she says, in a monotone, "but you still want me?"

I am struck with paralysis, unsure of exactly how I've screwed this up. Have I offended her beloved orchard? Does she see me as inconsistent and unreliable, guilty of wasting her time? "Yes," I manage, but my voice is too high. "Jemima will be better with the orchard. I have a brown thumb. But I still think you're wonderful."

Her eyes gradually curl up at their edges again, and finally Bridgette is looking at me with all of the affection I could wish for. "I'd like that. Please do visit again soon; Carina will let you in."

And then she is kissing me in the middle of the field, one gloved hand and one bare against my cheeks, and I can feel the glorious curves and bones of her pressed against my torso through her dress.

Bridgette takes a moment to recover her breath when she breaks away. "There may be some surprises when you come back."

"I can handle them."

She winks in reply, almost imperceptibly. "I know you can."

I take my paces backwards towards the gate. This is only a temporary parting.

She looks at me as if I'm magic.

INHERITANCE

They tell me that taking the memory pill is when you really become an adult.

My friend Marie took it when she was sixteen, as soon as she legally could, and then she stopped liking any of the guys our age or laughing at our favourite shows. That scared me for a long time. She promised she was fine, but there was something different in her eyes afterwards, like she was haunted.

Mum's had my pill ready for a while, ever since gran died. It contains most of my grandmother's memories, and my great-grandmother's, and my great-great grandmother's from when they first invented the technology. Mum says no pressure, but I know that it's supposed to give me perspective; give me experience to help me navigate my adult life, and make good choices.

Twenty-four is pretty old, but I think I'm finally ready. To be haunted.

The memories of my ancestors flood through me, overwhelming. Celebrations, funerals, childbirth, regrets, moments of joy and inertia. Life is long and life is short, and I will live my own with a legacy inside of me.

Mum hands me a lemonade to sip. "Do you regret it?" she asks.

Not at all.

MARINA, HEL AND CADY SAVE THE UNIVERSE

Marina turned eighteen exactly one week after her final high school exams had finished, which was the perfect time for a party. Her parents provided a modest amount of alcohol, allowed her to pre-make some raspberry and lime jelly shots, and then retired to their bedroom at 8:00 PM, partially to give Marina's guests some privacy and partially to get in some early napping.

Marina had organised a unicorn piñata, a chocolate fountain with multicoloured marshmallows, and wrapped a pass-the-parcel with condoms and tampons inside. She and her friends ate raw cookie dough off the cutting board and took selfies licking the knife. Marina wore an early birthday present from her mother: a pink satin cocktail dress patterned with black bat silhouettes, with ribbon bows to tie at the ends of the short sleeves. Her nails were a crisp pastel pink to match her lipstick, and her hair was clipped back with silver skull pins.

By 1:00 AM most of her guests had departed, and when Marina woke the next morning at close to 10:00 AM, the first thing she noticed were her skull clips shining on the faux wooden floor.

She had been asleep face-down on the couch cushions and now wiped a glob of drool from where it had been congealing on the side of her mouth. The wet patch of saliva on the couch would dry. She was alone, although the worst of the party mess looked like it had been taken care of. Her parents hadn't woken her, which seemed improbable bordering on suspicious.

Then she spotted the hole in the ceiling.

It was a neat square of light in the corner of their open-plan living area, near the kitchen benches. A small white ladder extended into the room, perhaps a metre and a half long. As Marina approached she saw tiny particles sparkle as they dropped past the rungs, collecting in small mounds on the kitchen tiles: fine, glittering, pale grains of sand.

She looked up, and had to glance away and back again. The sunlight was so bright. Through the hole was a clear blue sky with sunset-pink clouds and the edge of a palm frond. A sea bird was circling overhead and a feather floated lazily down to brush against Marina's cheek. And all the while the pale sand was still trickling, grain by grain, down the edges of the hole.

Marina fumbled for her phone, which was still in a pocket of her satin dress, and texted Hel and Cady: "You will want to come to mine NOW." She took a couple of photos of the ceiling hole, one up close and one from further away for context, and sent those through, too.

Hel texted back a string of question marks, and Cady wrote, "Are you still drunk?" but they both came. They had all been best friends since Year 9 English class and lived less than twenty minutes' walk from one another, so Marina didn't have to wait long.

While she was waiting Marina cleaned herself up with some facial wipes and pulled some silver sneakers on. The sound of the vacuum started upstairs, and she found her mother vacuuming the sunroom, even though it hadn't been used last night and Marina thought the carpet already looked fine.

"Mum, have you seen the hole above the kitchen?"

Her mother switched off the vacuum and Marina repeated the question.

"The hole?" Her mother appeared to think for a moment. "Oh, yes. Don't worry about that. We'll get it fixed soon."

"Fixed?" said Marina. "Are we talking about the same hole? The one with the beach in it?"

"Yes," said her mother, smiling and reaching for the power button again. "It's not important, Marina."

Marina took the steps down a little off-kilter. Usually her mother was deeply unsettled by a chip in their coffee table or their new shower door getting installed upside down. Her dad was trimming trees in the backyard and had equally noncommittal and unhelpful things to say about the hole. Just as Marina was seriously starting to consider if she'd lost her mind, the doorbell rang.

Helena was a plump, half-Greek, half-English seventeen-year-old wearing a black t-shirt, black leggings and a wicked grin. She still had traces of last night's eyeliner smudged under her eyes, and had her huge school backpack slung over her shoulders even though it looked wildly out of place without their usual uniform.

Cady had dyed her hair deep red on the last day of semester and wore it in two neat braids down to her collarbones. She had sharp green eyes behind black-rimmed glasses, and today she'd chosen a white t-shirt under flattering blue overalls.

Cady was four months older than Marina, and Marina thought she was easily the most gorgeous girl in their class. The other students couldn't see it because Cady never wore makeup and cared much more about physics, sci-fi and video games than current trends, but Marina thought she was perfect.

"Come on then," said Hel, blowing out a radioactive green bubble of gum. "Let's see it!"

Marina climbed the ladder first, feeling the heat of the sun break over her scalp once she'd breached the ceiling. When her shoulders cleared she pressed her fingers into the hot, glittering sand and stared.

The ocean was almost perfectly transparent, with just a slight hint of blue, like someone had added a few drops of food dye. Dozens of crabs waddled in the shallows, their shells shining pastel pink and blue, and Marina could see flashes of vibrant tropical fish in the waters beyond. The beach itself, which was quite narrow, was lined with palm trees draped with flowering candy-coloured vines, and pastel toucans and hummingbirds darted between them.

To Marina, it looked like paradise.

Hel and Cady followed behind her, brushing the sand off their knees.

"Holy shit," said Hel. "When did this happen?" She had a limited tolerance for loud parties and had left slightly after 11:00 PM. Cady liked them even less, and had slipped out the door around 10:15 after hugging Maria goodnight.

"I don't know," said Marina. "I think I fell asleep after 2:00 and there wasn't a hole then."

Cady shaded her eyes with her fingers. "It's alarming and unnatural," she said, looking more sceptical than disturbed, "but while we're here..." She approached a palm tree slowly, like one might approach a skittish cat, and held out her arm. Within fifteen seconds a hummingbird had flitted over, its wings a blur of speed, and alighted on her palm. Cady gave a little murmur of happiness. "I like this part."

After they had all touched the hummingbirds and picked the flowers and tucked the stems in each other's hair, Cady decided it was time to go home. Hel wanted to search for empty crab shells and Marina wanted to see what was further down the beach, but in the end the discussion was moot. The hole leading back to Marina's kitchen was gone. They dug their hands around where they thought the hole should have been, but there was only sand all the way down.

Hel had turned a little red and Cady had gone quite pale.

"Don't worry," said Marina, sensing the edge of an emotional precipice. "We'll find our way home soon. No-one ever gets to stay in magical places like this for long, right?"

They stayed a little less than twenty-four hours.

The sun was getting lower in the afternoon sky, even though it had been morning in Marina's living room. They had been walking roughly south along the beach for about half an hour, with Hel providing a steady monologue of complaints, vaguely related questions, and completely unrelated commentary about her favourite cartoon *Graveyard Business*. Cady, who usually looked so stoic that Marina struggled to read her, had been crying silently for most of the journey, her crumpled face turned away towards the sea.

Marina wished that she knew something to say or do to make Cady feel a little better. Just as she was starting to feel truly useless, there came a flurry of palm fronds to their left, and a particularly thick pink vine unwrapped itself from around a tree trunk. It dropped at their feet, actually a long, candy-floss-coloured cat that looked like it had been stretched out like a noodle, easily four times as long as the cats they were used to. It offered them shelter inside its nest in a large, hollowed-out palm tree, and described how much they reminded it of The Crying Girl.

No-one knew where she had come from, only that she was so giant that Marina's whole body could lie across one of her fingers, and that she would not stop crying. She did not appear to need to eat, or drink, or sleep, and within three weeks she had already turned the forest in a five-kilometre radius around her into a rotting marsh. If she were allowed to continue, before long The Crying Girl would drown the entire world.

All attempts to either calm her or attack her had been unsuccessful, explained the very long cat as Marina, Hel and Cady were settling inside his nest. But they looked so much like her; maybe they could help.

Now, Marina, Hel and Cady were no strangers to crying, and particularly in being persuaded not to do it. By the time they were in their late teens, instead of crying Marina had learnt to plaster on a convincing smile, Hel was ready with a hundred sharp rebukes, and Cady's face turned glacially cold until she was somewhere private or simply couldn't hide it anymore. They trekked to find The Crying Girl, but they didn't ask her to stop crying. They sat on The Crying Girl's shoulders and directed her back to the beach they'd arrived at, and asked her to cry in the ocean from now on. She might still end up drowning the world eventually, but the situation seemed better than the day before.

The hole in the sand had opened again, but it didn't look like it led directly to Marina's kitchen anymore. There was dark asphalt and a curb and what appeared to be a nature strip, and when Cady stuck her head and shoulders through with the other girls holding her legs for safety, she confirmed that she saw the Williams' garden with its orange roses and little white dog, which was only a couple of minutes walk from Hel's townhouse.

The three of them had a short but emotional argument about how to proceed. Marina was worried that if they left now they would never be able to come back to her paradise again. Hel had a hundred complaints about the magical world, but a thousand about their usual one. And Cady said that they had families and responsibilities back home, and that they knew nothing about what the new world was, not really, and that it was utterly imperative that *they did not stay*.

In the end, Cady kissed the inside of Marina's wrist and made her lower herself through the hole first, which Marina did with the great reluctance of someone forced to wake from an exquisite dream.

The three of them were soon sprawled across the Willams' nature strip and feeling like warmed-up roadkill. The physical change from the beach to the street had been immediate and undeniable. Marina had never had a hangover, but she thought this must be similar. She had an oppressive headache and her throat was so dry it was like someone had attacked it with a hair dryer. Her whole body ached like she had the flu, she was desperately thirsty, and she thought she might be hungry, too, if the rest of her wasn't feeling so pitiful.

They all staggered back to Hel's nearby townhouse, latched onto the water taps and the contents of Hel's fridge, and then promptly fell, exhausted, into sleep.

Marina woke on the hardwood floors of Hel's kitchen. Sweat had caked her satin birthday dress against her skin. Although she only had a limited idea of what time they'd arrived, several hours seemed to have passed, and she could hear the shower running. In the living room, Hel's father was watching the football and drinking an elaborate-looking cocktail with a lime in it, which he would have probably had to step over her sleeping body to make.

She retreated before he could notice her and found Hel in her bedroom, clad only in some old cotton underwear. Hel was in the middle of tossing some clothes out of her closet and onto the blankets.

"We all stink of piss and my dad's lost his mind," said Hel. "Put that dress in the basket and I'll give you something clean."

Marina blinked and felt around the skirt of her dress, which did feel oddly stiff in an off-putting way. She still didn't feel *good*, but she was well enough to clumsily unzip herself and trade it for a loose white dress with an empire waist. "Who pissed on us?" she asked.

Hel frowned but then broke into raucous laughter. "Oh, who knows? Cady said she smelt it as soon as we dropped back to earth, so…"

Hel changed into a clean version of the exact outfit she'd been wearing earlier. Hel's father, whom Marina remembered as a no-nonsense businessman with a neat goatee, now apparently didn't care that his daughter's friends had passed out on his floor in the middle of the day, stinking up his pristine townhouse. He didn't care about the picture of the ceiling portal Hel had tried to show him, and had only reacted with mild annoyance when she'd pelted him with some wrapped-up cookie dough that she'd stolen from Marina's party.

"That reminds me," Hel said, and retrieved the rest of the cookie dough ball from her old trousers to slip it into the pocket of her new ones.

Marina eyed it sceptically. "Is that still safe to eat?"

Hel shrugged in that stubborn way of hers that meant she would never outwardly agree, and they were only saved from further discussion because Cady chose that moment to walk in with wet hair, wearing belted sports shorts and an oversized grey singlet, and Marina thought she looked gorgeous to the point of distraction.

Marina was immediately reminded of Cady's velvet-soft lips on her wrist and couldn't think of a single thing to say.

Instead, Cady said, "Hel, there's another portal in your atrium."

They commandeered a wooden chair to help raise them into the new hole in Hel's ceiling. Cady remained highly guarded, and only agreed to come on the pre-conditions that none of them would stay, and that they would ideally be inside for no more than five minutes before returning.

This new world was nothing like Marina's pastel beach paradise. It was the middle of the night, which by itself was unremarkable, but the darkness had a rich, almost tangible thickness that made Marina think it probably never got lighter than their own later dusks or earlier dawns. They had arrived next to a village, or perhaps it was large enough for a town. Soft lighting illuminated its buildings and inhabitants in the form of streetlights, kerosene lamps and thousands of candles ranging from tiny to the size of her family's water tank.

The inhabitants, at least the ones they could see, were animated human skeletons with shining, polished bones. And tucked into every corner and draped over every roof were hundreds of white lilies, though Marina couldn't smell a thing. Almost everything was monochrome, and nothing had a scent. Hel, who never ran unless she had to, squealed and practically danced towards the village where a group of skeletons appeared to be talking, reading, and massaging liquid candle wax over their bones.

Marina and Cady hung back and observed with wary interest, but Hel soon jogged back with a sizable grin. "They're thrilled to see us, you guys!" she reported. "They need humans to convert the flesh bodies they receive into just the bones, and the few humans who pass through are usually too squeamish to do it!"

"Where... Where do they get the bodies from?" asked Marina, but her friends either ignored her or didn't hear.

Cady's eyebrows had furrowed so thoroughly it was like someone had pulled them together with stitches. "We can't *stay*, Hel, remember? This was a brief visit only, and I'm certainly not pulling wet flesh away from corpses..."

As she spoke, she'd been retreating carefully towards where the hole had been, and where they soon discovered it wasn't any longer. There was only the rich, loamy soil beneath their feet.

Cady swore extensively under her breath and looked truly angry for the first time Marina remembered in a long while.

Marina twisted her hands inside her cotton pockets. "We do the quest and we go home, okay?"

Hel beamed at her, and Cady scowled, and the three of them approached the waiting skeletons.

There were, Marina estimated, perhaps fifty dead bodies stacked waiting for them within the dedicated freezer room. They had been guided into a longish one-storey building which in their world she would've called the morgue, but here was called The Chrysalis, and even though it made sense in context the name combined with the chill made all the blonde hairs on the backs of her arms stand up.

Despite Marina's unease, processing the corpses grew repetitive after the first few. Two or three of them would haul a body from the freezer into what she thought of as the 'main room', which was a large square space with no windows and white tiles everywhere, including on the ceiling and across the door. They would light four large lanterns around the corpse, all of which smoked terribly and smelt of lavender and cinnamon, and wait a minute or two until the corpse's essence rose out of its body like a globule rising in a lava lamp. Once this had happened, one of them would catch the essence in a glass sphere and set it to one side with care, so that it looked like a glowing amber ball floating inside an upside-down fish-bowl.

Cady, who was resentful that bodily fluids existed at all, retreated to the far corner while Marina and Hel slipped their knives into the first couple of bodies. She was expecting a seeping, a splattering, and was instead filled with relief: in The Chrysalis, their gold-plated knives slipped past skin and muscle and marrow like soft clay, and the dead flesh fell off the bones in easy, dry wholes like rubber pieces pried off a mould.

The remaining skeletons always looked slightly off-colour against the stark white of the tiles. The three of them rubbed the bones with polishing clothes until they were smooth and shiny, and then held the goldfish bowl of essence over the skeleton until the glowing ball spiralled down and fused with the bones, shaking and re-orienting them on the floor like the skeleton was undergoing an electric shock. Once the bones had settled the skeleton would usually acknowledge them with a nod or a tip of its invisible hat, and then show itself calmly out of the door.

By the time they were down to the last two bodies, Marina was more than ready to go home.

And then there was a third body in the freezer room.

Somewhere around pulling the flesh off the previous corpse, Marina and Cady had lost track of Hel. Marina had thought that Hel had gone off to pee or something, but she was only sitting in the freezer room. She was stone cold and slumped like a doll against the other corpses, golden knife hanging from one hand and blood freezing across her chest where it had initially streamed out of the incision in her neck.

Marina yelped in shock and recoiled without thinking. She bumped into Cady, who had clocked the situation faster and stilled in the doorway. Hel was clearly dead, but Marina went through the motions regardless: calling Hel's name, checking for a pulse, checking for breath.

Marina turned to Cady when she was done. They were both shivering. "She wanted this."

"Yes." Cady's voice was monotone.

"So — we process her. She gets to stay in her paradise and be bones." Marina's fingers were going numb. She tucked them between her thighs for warmth, glancing at Cady's even face and then away.

"No," said Cady. "Normally I'd be torn, if this was what she really wanted. If she'd have a good life here. Or just something that wasn't her old life, if that was so intolerable. But this isn't a decision." Cady wasn't looking at Marina. Cady wasn't looking anywhere, but her voice still hit like a warhammer. "This isn't even real."

"Hel's dead," Marina said quietly. "How can you be so sure?"

They processed the last couple of bodies — the old corpses that weren't Hel's — in near silence. They watched the skeletons saunter away. Then they hoisted Hel's frozen body between the two of them — Marina's elbows under Hel's arms, Cady clutching Hel's ankles — and shuffled back to the dirt where the hole had been. It had parted in a loose square, and they could see a sunlit swimming pool shimmering through the gap. Somebody's well-kept garden. Some of the dirt had trickled through and was floating like an oil slick on the water.

"You think this will work?" Marina breathed, setting Hel's body down next to the hole.

"We'll see in a minute," said Cady. "You want to lower Hel down or receive her?"

Marina worried that she would drop the body on Cady's head. "Umm... Receive."

They guided Hel's body down. Marina struggled to hold herself upright in the water, the exhaustion and sickness dropping into her like a wave once she had cleared the mouth of the hole. And then mercifully, half-soaked in the swimming pool and with an uninjured neck, Hel stirred to life in Marina's arms.

"Fuck you," murmured Hel, and Marina couldn't summon up the energy to laugh.

They took longer to recover this time. Cady's mother had left her front door unlocked and they ate, drank, slept, showered, and changed clothes multiple times before they felt mostly human again. Hel had ended up in a pair of Cady's loose black tracksuit pants, and had made a deliberate show of replacing the old, wrapped piece of cookie dough into their pockets while looking Marina and Cady in the eyes, like a cat pushing a full glass off a sideboard.

Marina's phone had drowned in the swimming pool, but when she called her parents from Cady's landline they were so unresponsive that she may've been better off speaking to an answering machine. Hel's phone was somewhat waterproof, but even once she'd recharged it there were no messages from her father. Cady's mother seemed to have settled permanently in her living room, cross-stitching and watching documentaries about steamboats. No-one seemed to care where they had been or that they'd recently felt like bird shit smeared across a car window.

Cady had taken it the worst of the three of them, cross-legged and almost catatonic on the couch near her mother, who had started to hum the soundtrack from The Sound of Music. Marina brought Cady a hot chocolate she hadn't asked for and probably wouldn't drink, and in an effort to make Cady's eyes focus out of the middle distance, Marina said: "You know there's a hole in your bedroom ceiling."

They each stood on a milk crate on top of Cady's denim bedcovers and poked their heads into the hole, just for a few seconds.

"I'm not going in there," declared Hel. "It's just your boring bedroom, exactly like this one, but with more dogs and cats." Marina had spotted a bulldog by the bookcase and a Tonkinese on the windowsill.

"Yes," said Cady, monotone. "It's the best one." When neither Hel nor Marina said anything else to fill the silence, her face contorted. "I went with both of you into your stupid places! You won't come with me for one minute into mine!"

Marina dug her pastel pink nails into her palms. "I'll go with you," she said.

"No, don't bother." Cady strode off into the hall, and then paused just outside the doorway to take an audible breath. "We shouldn't go, of course," she clarified. It sounded like she was forcing herself to be calm. "It's just not fair. That mine's last."

Hel and Marina found Cady in the attic, afternoon light illuminating dust motes in front of dark wooden walls, where she had pointed her telescope firmly to the west.

Marina had been expecting to apologise, but Cady beckoned them over without taking her eyes from the square window, so their transgressions had either been forgiven or superseded.

"Look," said Cady, "They're not even trying to hide it. It's just out there in the open like a blister."

Marina and Hel hustled to follow her line of sight. They didn't even need the telescope. A large dome, perhaps the size of 300 or 400 apartments piled together, had appeared on the horizon, like a Godzilla-sized kid had dropped it unceremoniously on the usual skyline. Through the telescope lens they could see its smoothness, the shine of the metallic gunmetal grey, the occasional dots of colour around its sides that might be windows or lights or mechanics.

"That wasn't there last week," Cady said. "At first I thought we weren't back in the real world, but no — this is just like that episode of *Galaxy Ship X*. I'm going down there."

Marina's mouth was too dry, like someone had just swabbed it with a handful of cotton buds. "It looks like a trap," she said, and then, "What are you expecting us to do?"

Hel said, "I don't know, I reckon life is better now than a week ago."

Cady's face displayed zero tolerance. "You don't have to come," she said. "But it's my mother. No-one messes with my mother."

In the end, all three of them went, and not entirely empty-handed. They took the supplies for two Molotov cocktails, courtesy of the kerosene bottles in Cady's mother's old camping gear, the rags from her gardening box, and the lighter that lived above their stove.

Cady drove them within shouting distance of the dome. The traffic was light, but the roads were far from deserted. From there they proceeded on foot, the bottles thumping and clinking in backpacks. Marina wiped clammy hands on the pair of distressed jeans she had borrowed.

As they approached, it became clear that there was a dark opening in the dome, just waiting there like a mouth in a dentist's office. It seemed unattended.

"Maybe they just think everyone's watching football," muttered Hel. Marina could see the radioactive green chewing gum squashed between Hel's teeth again. Earlier, Hel had ducked into a service station, picked up a packet of gum and a Coke in full view of the cashier, and then slowly backed out of the store to see if he objected.

He hadn't.

They edged towards the waiting mouth of the dome. "Trap," Marina whispered under her breath, but they couldn't see an alternative. Cady squeezed Marina's shoulder. They stepped off the street and into the darkness.

There was an immediate shuffling, shifting sound behind them that made Marina think of a boulder sliding across an entrance. The lights flickered and came on, as if they were motion-controlled, and illuminated a large space perhaps a bit smaller than their school's assembly hall. Most of it was empty, with a rubbery lilac floor and a raised platform comprising the back half of the room, lined with what looked like vertical glass boxes. Hundreds of twenty-cent-sized dark marks dotted the floor, as if someone had repeatedly burned it with an oversized cigarette.

Marina turned to check the source of the shifting sound. A dozen identical guards blocked the entrance, all with the same dark visors covering the top half of their faces. Their expressions were neutral, unreadable; Marina couldn't tell if they were androids or organic or something else.

Their backpacks were taken away with brisk efficiency. Once the guards seemed satisfied that Marina, Hel and Cady posed no threat, they simply stood in perfect formation, completely blocking the entrance.

"They're waiting for something," said Marina.

It wasn't a long wait. From the other side of the room they heard a long swish, like the sweep of a gown or the lazy swoop of a raptor, and then a woman the size of a basketball player strode into the room, the trail of her dress flowing far out behind her like a red carpet.

In closer proximity, it was clear that 'woman' wasn't quite right: what Marina had initially thought was a headdress appeared to be an actual set of antlers growing out of the creature's skull, and they moved and twitched like a cat's tail. Above her two purple eyes her forehead split apart to reveal a third eye, and there were too many fingers attached to her palms.

"Thank you so much for the pleasure of your company," said the creature, with a rich voice like expensive coffee. "It's wonderful when your kind come to me, and save me the trouble."

Hel's loud laughter rang through the hall. When Marina glanced at her, Hel had one eyebrow cocked like a question mark, but her hands were shaking at her sides.

"What the shit?" said Hel. "Our kind?"

"Yes," said the creature, as if speaking to a small child. "I don't come to planets to destroy them, or to enslave. I simply have the population go about its business, so that they don't disturb me. Most of your brains are very similar to ours. We put something in the water. Something in select packaged foods, like butter or potato chips or cookie dough. The tiniest amount is enough. But sometimes those with slightly different brains aren't affected. Most of you die in the hallucinogenic pocket spaces I craft for you, but others find their way here, or cause trouble, so we pick them up."

The girls understood what she was referring to. Cady had been diagnosed with autism about eighteen months earlier, and they were 95% sure that Hel was autistic, too, although her father refused to have her tested. When Marina took the online tests she always scored right on the borderline between neurotypical and autistic, which she had never known quite what to do with, but she'd never been more thankful for being a bit different.

The creature steepled its too-many fingers. "I won't kill you, of course; we simply put you on ice until you won't be a problem any more."

Marina's eyes followed the creature's gesture to the edge of the room. With more context, she could see that the glass boxes towards the back of the platform weren't empty at all. They were filled with shapes and colours that were probably people.

"How..." Marina cleared her throat. "How long would we stay in there for?"

The creature's antlers spread in what Marina guessed was the equivalent of a shrug. "Between a few months and forever."

Marina, Hel and Cady glanced at each other. Hel swallowed her gum and then appeared to be gagging for a second, and the other girls saw a light spark inside her eyes: Hel had a plan, and they thought they had an approximate understanding of what that would be.

Cady, who was the least comfortable with lying, crossed her arms under her breasts. "I'll go first," she said.

The creature nodded. "Very good," she said. "Just..." Its antlers swivelled slightly, and a beam of purple light shot out from one of the branches to singe the floor inches from Cady's feet. "Don't be foolish."

Cady nodded. She walked up the ramp to the platform slowly, and allowed the creature to tuck her into one of the nearest glass boxes like a doll in its new packaging.

Marina bit her own tongue like a pacifier. She kept half an eye on Hel while trying to be subtle about it: the way Hel's hand had disappeared into her pants pocket for a moment, the way it had then found its way into Hel's mouth so Hel could 'bite her nails'. Marina had thought that Hel might have given her the cookie dough, instead, in the guise of holding her hand, but this could work, too.

Once the creature had sealed Cady into the box with a hiss like air leaving an airlock, she swivelled back to Marina and Hel. Hel had her thumbs tucked into her waistband with a practised arrogance; Marina hoped it only had to be half-convincing.

"I'll go," said Hel, "but I'm seventeen and I don't want to be frozen and never been kissed." She grinned, charming and predatory in a way Marina thought the creature might understand. "I want to kiss you on my way out."

The creature studied Hel with narrowed eyes. Marina thought she might vomit from the stress. Finally, the creature laughed and said, "Fine," and crooked a finger in Hel's direction.

Hel sauntered up to the platform and landed an awkward kiss on the creature's mouth. She was obviously trying, but the kiss lasted no more than three or four seconds. Marina desperately hoped it was enough.

Once Hel had been sealed away, too, Marina was the only one left, and it felt like all the air had been sucked from the room.

Praying for the cookie dough to take effect soon, Marina tried to stall with additional questions (*What are you here to do?* and *How did you make our portals so perfect?*) but it seemed that the creature was done talking. Finally, Marina blurted out, "I want to kiss you, too! I'm very good. Hel got to kiss you."

The creature sighed but agreed, as if it was an imposition. Marina raised herself up on her toes, wrapped her hands around the back of the creature's neck, and kissed her like she was in the Olympics of kissing. Like the universe depended on it, which it quite possibly did. The creature tasted like lime and frankincense. Marina kissed the creature until her toes ached, until she could barely keep herself upright any more.

Finally, the creature's body seemed to slacken a little, and Marina allowed her heels to drop to the floor again. "Why don't you and your guards go back into the centre of the ship for a while," Marina suggested, eyes wide, "and then leave Earth in about, like, half an hour?"

She was mostly expecting laughter or a laser hole in the forehead, but the creature just nodded vacantly and wandered back the way she had come, and Marina was so flooded with relief that her knees buckled.

Marina stumbled over to Cady's box and studied Cady's cold, still face through the glass. Ice had begun to build on her thick eyelashes. Marina quickly gripped the lever and opened the seal.

It was freezer-cold inside, but hadn't been for so long that Cady didn't open her eyes when the glass opened. Marina wrapped her arms around Cady's waist and pulled her free, trying to warm her stiff frame with her body heat.

"You did it," Cady said, frosty lips close to Marina's ear.

"I did," said Marina. Then, "It was a team effort." Before she could lose her nerve, she added, "Can I kiss you now?"

Cady was starting to be able to move her arms and legs again. "Free everyone else first, you dick." But it didn't sound unkind. Marina heard the 'first', and grinned, and rushed to empty all of the glass boxes, beginning with Hel.

AS LONG AS WE BOTH SHALL LIVE AND AFTER, TOO

Before she dies to save us both, my wife shears off a chunk of her hair, thrusts it into my hands and tells me to take care of the cat.

I am not the type to remarry. Eventually, once the veil of grief has lifted somewhat, I downsize. Half of my wife's possessions, I absorb into my own. A quarter, I box away. A quarter I give to her family, to friends, to charity. I throw myself into my work. I grow accustomed to quiet evenings with the cat in front of the TV.

I skim the science magazines at the library. I am not an optimist by any means, but a tiny part of me begins to whisper: *maybe, maybe.*

Years pass. The cat dies.

I purchase an android body. When my wife was alive, we were comfortable enough with money if we budgeted strictly. Since she died, I've earned multiple promotions and spent little; I can afford a higher-end model. I start with the body of twenty-four-year-old me, and make all the little changes that I've wished for forever: smaller nose, smaller breasts, remove the moles and freckles. But I don't change so much that my wife wouldn't recognise me.

When my wife has been dead for twenty-three years, human cloning has advanced enough that I take out the lock of human hair, the last gift she gave me. Some of our old mutual friends have synthetic bodies, a great respect for my wife, and desire a child. They raise her clone as their daughter: she is granted a new name, new birth year, new life.

I can't be her parent; I can't even visit, or she'll see me as one of the old people she knew since she was little. I send gifts, though – for her new birth date and Christmas and whenever else I can get away with:

Congratulations on your first day of school!
Congratulations on losing your first tooth!
Congratulations on passing your piano exam!

I send books and movies and toys I remember my wife talking about from her childhood, in addition to more modern ones I think she might enjoy. If I send anything from my wife's boxes, I make sure it's nothing that will break my heart if it's lost or broken. Later, I add clothes and jewellery and gadgets to the mix. I sign all the gifts 'love,' and my real name.

Her parents send me photos – just the 2D, non-moving ones, I insist – and her thank you messages, as if she is a child I'm sponsoring overseas. It is an intensely strange situation. Still, the growing voice whispers: *maybe, maybe.*

I watch her grow up whilst my body never grows older. I wish I could hold her hand when she breaks her ankle, when she loses out on the job she wanted, when she's broken up with again. *Please, please, don't find anyone better than me.*

I wait. I am old, and I am patient.

I wait until she is twenty-two. *Forgive me*, I think, *for not telling you earlier. Forgive me for not telling you later. Forgive me for telling you at all.*

The restaurant we had our first date at, decades ago, has shut down, so I pick something similar I have scoped out in advance. I wear an updated version of the outfits she always used to like, and arrive half an hour early because I can't stand the thought of getting there after her.

I pat the photos in my pocket. I will spread them out in front of her and say, "Look: this is me and my wife."

She walks in seven minutes early. She is my wife and not my wife: a different generation, different experiences, but similar enough. She is wearing the golden heart necklace I sent her years ago.

I wave to her; she spots me and smiles. It is not the kind of smile I remember, the kind that says *I love you, this is safe, you are mine forever*, but it could be one day, my heart says. Maybe, maybe.

TRACES OF US, HOT ENOUGH FOR DINNER

Terribly rude of Georgia and Tim to get married on the first anniversary of my fiancée's death.

When I wake on the 14th of April there's already a text from my mother: I have to promise I'll arrive in time for the ceremony or they'll swing by on the way and physically bundle me into the car.

I squint in the sunlight and unpeel myself from the torso-sized pool of sweat on the fitted sheet.

All I actually want to do today is linger in bed, take an extended shower, and then take tulips to the place where Lucy bled out in her car a year ago. Instead, I tap back, '*Fine,*' and rifle through my closet for something acceptable to wear for this damn wedding.

I settle on a kelly green dress with a mesh collar and mesh sleeves. Most of my lone tattoo is visible through the sleeves: the speech-bubble rectangle of Lucy's last text: '*See you soon! Love you!*' Mum will say some variant of "That's hideously morbid" when she sees it, but she's welcome to.

I tuck on some shoes, brush my teeth and paint on some lipstick. Then I stand frozen in a sunspot until I can bear to step outside.

Georgia and Tim's wedding is like most other weddings until we reach the reception dinner. You know the kind: they meet each other's minimum expectations (his are high, hers are low) and they'll raise kids together, but there's nothing about the ceremony or speeches that are particularly personal, that says *you're my soulmate* or that imply that thousands of other people wouldn't do just as good a job in the roles of their husband or wife.

But the dinner mixes it up. Just as the waiter is serving me my shrivelled quail, the floor-length windows in front of us shatter, and in pour dozens of monsters – *demons*, I think. Child-size and muscular and lean, in all of the colours of obsidian and charcoal and dusky blood. Sharp eyes and sharp claws and sharp teeth. They descend on the wedding guests like a wave, and there is barely time for any running or shrieking before they are fully upon us.

I see swirls of frantic glitter and sequins, and crockery and glassware upended into the air, and then the shining points of demonic teeth before they sink into my jugular.

Fuck Georgia and Tim.

When I wake on the 14th of April there's already a text from my mother. I sit on the bed cradling my phone, trying to shrug off the nightmare of the violently interrupted wedding reception.

When my heartbeat finally slows, I text back '*Fine*' and pull on the kelly green dress.

The ceremony is exactly the way I remember it. When I arrive, Mum scolds me for my unbrushed hair and the existence of my tattoo, and she's showing off the infinity brooch Dad gave her for their 20th wedding anniversary. The church aisle is steeped in that new biodegradable glitter: white and silver. Georgia walks in to Kings of Leon's 'Use Somebody,' which is a very questionable choice, and carries a bouquet of waratahs. The priest talks for seemingly hours, and my brother Jason's hands keep twitching towards the 3DS in his suit jacket pocket. The bride and groom say the standard vows. My sister Tamsin loses one of her hoop earrings under the pews and never gets it back.

By the time we've all filed out into the car park there are sizable sweat stains on my dress, and my mind is overwhelmed with visions of demons filling the reception hall next door.

"Mum," I say, tugging on her sleeve with shaking fingers. "Please can we go home? I don't feel well at all."

"Amber," she whisper-hisses. "You will not ruin this day for us."

"I'm not trying to ruin it," I say, and promptly throw up onto the nature strip.

Tamsin hands me a handful of tissues from her handbag.

"Please," I say. "I'd drive myself home, but I don't think I can manage it."

The four of us climb into my mother's four-wheel-drive. Jason is much happier playing on his 3DS, and Tamsin is only a little irritated that she won't get the chance to flirt with the boys at the reception, and I feel my entire body starting to unwind as we drive away from the scene of demon apocalypse 2019.

Back at the family home, Mum bakes us our favourite lasagne and sends Jason and me out to fetch parsley while Tamsin sets the table. Jason's 3DS screen is a bright spot in the garden as the last sliver of sun dawdles above the horizon. I settle my hand on his shoulder to help guide him as we near the parsley patch near the river.

But there are other spots of light in the garden. My fist tightens around Jason's shoulder, and the other reaches around to flick his 3DS screen closed. He starts to protest until he sees them too, dozens of shining eyes around us getting closer and closer: white and red and silver pairs, emerging in a rough circle around us. Demons with goat's horns or four arms or mouths gaping out of their palms. They're high in the trees and enmeshed in the shrubbery and rising out of the grasses.

They creep up around us until there is no alternative ending, and then they leap as one.

#

When I wake on the 14th of April there's already a text from my mother. I barely resist the urge to hurl my phone at the opposite wall. How am I supposed to reply? *Can't go, mum, demons will eat me.*

I sit on the linoleum and guzzle half a 1.25-litre bottle of Diet Coke. Then I pull on my tracksuit pants over my sleeping shirt, text back '*See you there*' and haul ass over to the local Bunnings.

I tear into the church parking lot just as the ceremony is finishing. Mum has been blowing up my phone for the past hour and looks incensed to see me finally arriving in a hired ute piled high with wooden planks. "Mum!" I shout. "Tamsin! Jason! Get in the car right now! This is fucking life and death! *Get in the goddamned car!*"

To their credit, my siblings glance at each other and jog towards the rear doors.

My mother reaches for Tamsin's arm but is too slow. "Amber..." she starts, but I yell, "I'll explain in the *motherfucking car*, mum!" and she sighs and climbs in.

On the drive to our family home I relate the minor details of Georgia and Tim's wedding ceremony, which they have just experienced, and then the details of the pre-dinner chunk of the wedding reception, which they have not, ending with the slaughter of every guest to a small army of demonic wedding crashes. I narrate our failed lasagne at home and my plan to barricade us all inside my childhood bedroom (now Mum's home gymnasium feat. my Lady Gaga curtains she never replaced).

Pausing impatiently at a red light, I examine their suspicious faces. "Look," I say. "I don't really care if you don't believe me. Do this one thing for me today, and I swear if nothing happens I'll patch up the room, I'll go to therapy if you want, Mum, I'll get my tattoo lasered off, Tasmin can have my car, and Jason, I don't know what you want, I'll help you hit on girls or something. Okay?"

Fuckin' okay.

We nail up Mum's gym so nice and tight with the wooden planks. Nice solid wood, nice solid nails, not an inch of door or windows uncovered. We have a small pile of food and drink stacked on the running machine, in case we're stuck here for a while, and a crowbar propped against the weightlifting bench so we can pry ourselves free. Honestly, even if they think I'm a nutcase, I haven't felt this close to my family in years.

I check my watch. "Not long until sundown now." I take up the crowbar like a baseball bat and position myself in the middle of the room. It's hard to get the perfect grip with my sweaty hands. "Guys, if we don't live through this and I wake up and it's still April 14th tomorrow, what would convince you I was telling the truth? What's something I would never know otherwise?"

Jason doesn't take long to answer. "Just tell me your middle name is Rose."

"What? That's not something I don't know. That's not even the truth."

"It's a reference, Amber. Killer movie. I'll know what you're talking about."

I roll my eyes at him. "I don't— Fine. Tamsin?"

She's jack-knifed into a corner. "Um," she says, "I have a mole on my left boob. That no-one's ever seen, or knows about."

"Okay," I say, my eyes flicking between our wooden barricades. "Mum?"

I have to prompt her a second and third time. Eventually, she says, "I won a calligraphy contest when I was twenty-two. I wrote: *sometimes there are too many lilies in the house.*"

I sew all of these phrases deep into my brain matter.

The demons do come, of course. I am expecting banging when they do, but there is no banging. They slip through the negligible cracks between and under the pieces of wood like shadows, like liquid, like they are made of smoke or sand. The only noises come from our own trembling mouths, seeing the claws coalesce into their full forms as they slip into the room.

I leap into action, smashing the crowbar into the claws, but there is an ocean of them pouring in from where we tried to block off the door and windows, and I notice some are even slipping in through the bars of the five-inch air vent.

I swing the crowbar as fast as I can manage. I manage to knock three of them on their backs before I feel a pair of horns impale deep into my lower back and thrust me into the air like skewered meat.

I do try. It's not fair to say I didn't try.

I drive my family as far away as possible.

I put us on a boat. On a plane.

I seal us in an airlocked room.

The demons always, always come.

Maybe it's just me they want; I FaceTime Tamsin while we're suburbs apart, watching the demons cannonballing into her living room while they open my door with a protracted squeak and hold a quiet finger to their teeth.

Not just me, then.

I try to protect us in a shooting range, in a police station, I seal us in a ring of fire and gasoline.

The demons always come.

I don't always try.

I go to Georgia and Tim's wedding reception and write questionable poetry in Sharpie on their napkins:

> *Oh*
>
> *Well*
>
> *You're going to hell*
> *You'll never be cold*
> *And I'll be there*
>
> *:)*

I go to Georgia and Tim's wedding reception and get blackout drunk in the ladies toilets.

I go to Georgia and Tim's wedding reception, get slightly less drunk, and steal the microphone from the DJ's desk: "We were supposed to get married! Lucy and me!"

The DJ quickly mutes my microphone and cranks up the music, but joke's on him because I wrench out the electric plug for his equipment, and I have a loud voice from all the Speech & Drama classes Mum made me take in primary school. Speaking of, Mum has stood up and is making her way over to where I'm gesturing wildly in my kelly green dress. "We were supposed to get married last September!"

"Amber!" she hisses.

Fuck off, Mum. "We were going to marry in the botanic gardens," I continue. "Did you know that?" Everyone in the room is watching me. I clamber onto the faux-marble bar where Mum can't easily get to me.

"Amber, you're making a fool of yourself!"

"No," I say, "Lucy already did that when she went and fucking died." I curtsy to my audience. "And now Georgia and Tim are getting married on the anniversary of her not existing anymore. And why the hell should they be able to do that when they don't love each other one fraction of how much Lucy and I loved each other." My blood is drumming in my ears like a dirge. "And..."

At the other end of the room, the first of the waiters are backing into the dining room with the shrivelled quail.

"And why am I still here?" I whisper, drawing a chopping knife from the pockets of my cocktail dress. This isn't where I need to be, but there's no time to change today until tomorrow. For now, I declare in my fiercest battle cry, "Fuck Georgia and Tim!"

I slice the knife across my neck in one fluid stroke.

I linger in bed on the 14th of April, staring at the ceiling and focusing intently on the feeling of my breath entering and leaving my body.

There's already a text from my mother. *Sorry, I won't be here*, I write back, and then turn off my phone.

I take a shower, towel myself off and climb into my wedding dress. It's simple, ivory, lacy panels and asymmetric hem. When I drive towards the fanciest florist I know, it doesn't get in the way.

I purchase the most elaborate tulip arrangement. I bring it with me to the last place Lucy ever took a breath, and place it in the dirt there like an offering.

Then I wait in the car.

As the streetlamps are flickering to life, the demons slink out of the trees beside the highway. They surround the car gradually, stalking it like a prey animal, closing in their circle like a noose.

Some of them are already clawing the locked doors, the scraping sound of bone on metal, but that doesn't matter anymore. I see my love between their monstrous faces through the windshield. My Lucy, standing beside the highway in the pink dress with the tulip pattern, the one she wore to our first Valentine's Day.

The demons keep coming, always, always, breaking the glass and breaking my skin, but I see her in between their writhing bodies, standing so still, the breeze playing through her hair, and she's smiling, she's smiling at me with all the love in the universe.

See you soon! Love you!

The demons are a swarm inside the car. They're all over me, a mass of shredding and hunger, but tears of joy pour down my bloody cheeks.

I see her smile. I see her smile at me.

FANCY SOME MORE STORIES?

Thank you for reading *Pick Your Potion*! If you enjoyed your time here, please consider leaving a review on Goodreads, Amazon, or another site of your choice.

Did you know that Ephiny Gale has more than fifty published short stories and novelettes? Many of them are available to read in *Next Curious Thing*, her previous collection.

If you'd like to receive some **free stories** and find out when Ephiny has brand new fiction published, sign up to the newsletter at ephinygale.com

ABOUT EPHINY GALE

Ephiny Gale was born in Victoria, Australia, and is still there, alongside her lovely wife and a small legion of bookcases. She is the author of more than fifty published short stories and novelettes, which have appeared in publications including *PseudoPod, Constellary Tales,* and *Beneath Ceaseless Skies.* Her stories have won the Best of the Net award for fiction and have been finalists for multiple Aurealis Awards.

She has also written several produced stage plays and musicals, including the sold-out *How to Direct from Inside* at La Mama and *Shining Armour* at The 1812 Theatre. Her script *Time Scraps* was a finalist in St Martin's National Playwriting Competition, and *Hearts up Sleeves* won the Five Minute Play award at Dante's.

When not writing, Ephiny currently works as a Senior Project Manager for a website development company. Her previous roles have included: Executive Assistant; coordinating a major arts festival; Association Secretary for the Green Room Awards (Melbourne's premier performing arts awards); nine months as a professional wedding DJ; and working as an executive of a university student association.

Ephiny has a Masters in Arts Management, a red belt in taekwondo, and a passion for psychology, gaming, and storytelling in all its forms. She also especially enjoys Italian greyhounds, playing board games with friends, and eating raspberries in the sunshine.

More at ephinygale.com

CONTENT WARNINGS

While care has been taken, please note that this is not an all-inclusive list.

Mild instances and brief references to the following have also been listed beneath their categories for the sake of caution.

Animal abuse or significant injury to an animal
Faewild

Amputation or loss of body parts
CurioQueens; Faewild; La Vie En Mer; Light and Sleek and Strong; Marina, Hel and Cady Save the Universe; The Orchard; Traces of Us, Hot Enough for Dinner

Body horror
CurioQueens; Faewild; La Vie En Mer; Light and Sleek and Strong; Marina, Hel and Cady Save the Universe; The Magic in Our Hands; The Orchard; Traces of Us, Hot Enough for Dinner

Bullying
Faewild; Nowhere, Australia

Cancer
La Vie En Mer

Cannibalism vibes
La Vie En Mer; Light and Sleek and Strong

Child abuse or significant injury to a child
La Vie En Mer; Marina, Hel and Cady Save the Universe; Rewind; The Candle Queen; Traces of Us, Hot Enough for Dinner

Death of a loved one or close family member
All the Times I'm Ten; As Long as We Both Shall Live and After, Too;

CurioQueens; La Vie En Mer; Neuro; Overnight, a Forest Grew; Restoration; The Orchard; Traces of Us, Hot Enough for Dinner

Depression
La Vie En Mer; Marina, Hel and Cady Save the Universe; Neuro; Smol Animaux; Solace

Domestic violence
La Vie En Mer; Watchhouse

Drugs, drugging, or passing out
Marina, Hel and Cady Save the Universe; Overnight, a Forest Grew; The Candle Queen; Traces of Us, Hot Enough for Dinner; Watchhouse

Hate crime: queerphobia or ableism
Marina, Hel and Cady Save the Universe; Watchhouse

Homicide/murder
La Vie En Mer; Last Text; Rewind; Traces of Us, Hot Enough for Dinner; Watchhouse

Kidnapping or long-term separation of a child from their parents
All the Times I'm Ten; Faewild; Marina, Hel and Cady Save the Universe; Smol Animaux; The Candle Queen

Manipulation
Marina, Hel and Cady Save the Universe; Smol Animaux; Rewind; The Magic in Our Hands; The Most Powerful Witch in Witchville; Watchhouse

Physical violence
CurioQueens; Faewild; La Vie En Mer; Last Text; Nowhere, Australia; Traces of Us, Hot Enough for Dinner; Faewild

Plague or virus
All the Times I'm Ten; Light and Sleek and Strong; Marina, Hel and Cady Save the Universe; Smol Animaux; Solace; The Most Powerful Witch in Witchville

Sexual assault vibes
Nowhere, Australia

Suicide or suicidal references
Last Text; Light and Sleek and Strong; Marina, Hel and Cady Save the Universe; Rewind; The Magic in Our Hands; Traces of Us, Hot Enough for Dinner; Watchhouse; When the Ice Comes In

Torture or significant/extended physical suffering
La Vie En Mer; Marina, Hel and Cady Save the Universe; Rewind; Traces of Us, Hot Enough for Dinner

www.ingramcontent.com/pod-product-compliance
Lightning Source LLC
Chambersburg PA
CBHW031304120726
47906CB00003B/881